This book belongs to:

_____

_____

Five-Minute Stories

Cover illustrated by Sara Gianassi

First published 2017 by Parragon Books, Ltd.
Copyright © 2018 Cottage Door Press, LLC
5005 Newport Drive, Rolling Meadows, Illinois 60008
All Rights Reserved

10 9 8 7 6 5 4 3 2 1

ISBN: 978-1-68052-406-2

Parragon Books is an imprint of Cottage Door Press, LLC.
Parragon Books® and the Parragon® logo are
registered trademarks of Cottage Door Press, LLC.

Five-Minute Stories

Parragon®

Contents

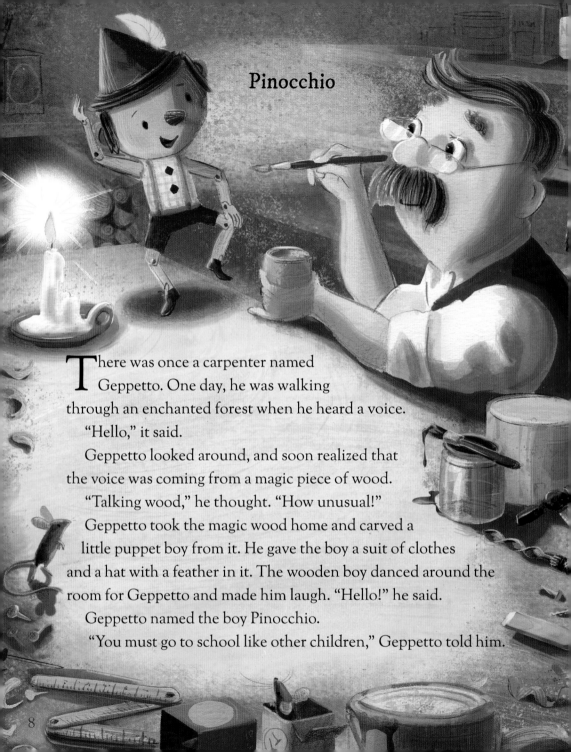

Pinocchio

There was once a carpenter named Geppetto. One day, he was walking through an enchanted forest when he heard a voice.

"Hello," it said.

Geppetto looked around, and soon realized that the voice was coming from a magic piece of wood.

"Talking wood," he thought. "How unusual!"

Geppetto took the magic wood home and carved a little puppet boy from it. He gave the boy a suit of clothes and a hat with a feather in it. The wooden boy danced around the room for Geppetto and made him laugh. "Hello!" he said.

Geppetto named the boy Pinocchio.

"You must go to school like other children," Geppetto told him.

So the next morning, Pinocchio skipped off to school on his wooden legs.

As he went along, a cricket hopped up onto his shoulder.

"You look like you could use a friend," he told Pinocchio. "I will help you learn right from wrong."

A little farther down the road, Pinocchio met a fox and a cat. They had heard the sound of lunch money jingling in his pocket.

"Don't bother going to school," said the fox. "Come and play with us instead!"

Pinocchio, not knowing any better, thought that sounded like a good idea.

"I don't think you are doing the right thing," the cricket told him. "You promised your father you would go to school."

But Pinocchio paid no attention to the cricket.

The cat and the fox led Pinocchio into a dark forest. "If you plant money here, it will grow into a money tree," they told him. "Just come back tomorrow, and you'll see."

"That doesn't sound right," said the cricket. "That money was for your lunch."

But Pinocchio didn't listen. He dug a hole in the ground and buried the coins in it.

Then Pinocchio went home, feeling very hungry. He did not tell his father that he hadn't been to school.

The next morning, Pinocchio didn't go to school either. Instead, with the cricket on his shoulder, he skipped into the forest to find his money tree.

When Pinocchio reached the spot where he'd buried his coins, there was no money tree. He dug down to look for the coins he had planted, but they were gone.

"The fox and the cat have played a trick on you," said the cricket. "They just wanted to get your money."

Pinocchio felt rather silly, but he pretended he didn't care. He stomped off into the forest.

"I'm going on an adventure," he said.

The little cricket begged him to go back to Geppetto, but Pinocchio walked on until it was dark and he was a little scared.

Soon they came to a tiny cottage. Pinocchio ran to the door and knocked loudly. A pretty fairy with turquoise hair answered the door.

"We're lost," explained Pinocchio. "Please can you help us?" The fairy invited them in and gave them some food.

"Why are you so far from home?" she asked kindly.

Pinocchio did not want to tell her that he had disobeyed his father.

"I was chased by a giant!" he lied.

Suddenly, Pinocchio's nose grew a little.

"The giant was taller than the trees ..." continued Pinocchio.

Pinocchio's nose grew some more.

"And I ran into the forest to escape!" he continued.

And Pinocchio's nose grew again!

He touched it in wonder.

"I have put a spell on you!" said the fairy. "Every time you tell a lie, your wooden nose will grow."

Pinocchio began to cry. How he wished he had gone to school as his father had said!

"I won't tell any more lies," promised Pinocchio.

The fairy called some friendly woodpeckers who pecked at Pinocchio's long nose until it was back to the way it used to be.

In the morning, Pinocchio rushed back through the forest with the little cricket perched on his shoulder.

"From now on I will do just as Father tells me," he said. But when he got home, Geppetto wasn't there. Instead, there was a note on the kitchen table.

Dear Pinocchio,
I have gone to look for you. I miss you, my son.
Your loving father, Geppetto.

Pinocchio was very sad. He knew he had caused a lot of trouble.

"We must find my father and bring him home," he sobbed. So he and the cricket set off again at once.

They began their search down by the river. Pinocchio stood too near the edge of the water, and he fell in with a **SPLASH!** The cricket jumped in to help him, but they were both swallowed by an enormous fish.

There, in the fish's tummy, they found Geppetto!

Pinocchio hugged his father tightly. "I won't leave you again!" he said.

The clever wooden boy took the feather from his hat and tickled the fish.

"A ... a ... a ... chooo!" The fish gave a mighty sneeze, and Geppetto, Pinocchio, and the cricket shot back out through the fish's mouth and landed on the bank of the river.

That night, when Pinocchio was tucked into his own little bed fast asleep, the fairy with turquoise hair flew in through his window.

"You are a good, brave boy," she said as he slept. And she kissed him on the forehead.

When Pinocchio awoke the next morning, he found that he was no longer made from wood. He was a real boy! From then on he was always a good son to Geppetto and the best of friends with the cricket, who didn't need to tell him right from wrong ever again.

The End

The Gingerbread Man

Once upon a time, a little old woman and a little old man lived by themselves in a little old cottage. One day the little old woman decided to bake a treat for the little old man.

"I'll make him a special gingerbread man," she thought.

She mixed all the ingredients together, rolled out the dough, cut out the gingerbread man, and popped him in the oven to bake.

Soon a delicious smell filled the little old cottage.

The little old woman was just putting on her oven mitts to check her baking, when she heard a strange voice calling out.

"Let me out! I've finished baking, and it's hot in here!"

The little old woman looked around. She was confused. "I must be hearing voices!" she chuckled to herself.

She opened the oven door and nearly fell over in surprise when the little gingerbread man jumped up off the baking pan, rushed past her, and ran out through the front door.

"Come back," cried the little old woman. "You smell delicious. We want to eat you!"

But the gingerbread man was too fast for the little old woman. He ran into the garden and past the little old man.

"Stop!" cried the little old man, setting down his wheelbarrow. "I want to eat you!"

But the little gingerbread man was already halfway down the road outside the little old cottage. He was very fast, and the little old woman and the little old man were very slow.

"Stop! Stop!" they wheezed, out of breath, as they ran down the road.

The gingerbread man darted under a fence into a field, singing as he went:

**"Run, run, as fast as you can,
You can't catch me, I'm the gingerbread man!"**

As the gingerbread man ran through the field, he passed a pig.

"Stop!" snorted the pig. "I want to eat you!"

"I've run away from a little old woman and a little old man, and I can run away from you," he said.

And he ran even faster, followed by the little old woman, the little old man, and the pig.

Soon the little gingerbread man met a cow.

"You smell scrumptious!" mooed the cow. "Stop, little man, I want to eat you!"

But the gingerbread man just ran faster. "I've run away from a little old woman, a little old man, and a pig, and I can run away from you," he cried.

The cow started to run after the gingerbread man, but he sprinted past her through the tall grass in the field, singing out:

"Run, run, as fast as you can,
You can't catch me, I'm the gingerbread man!"

The little old woman, the little old man, the pig, and the cow ran and ran, but none of them could catch the little gingerbread man.

In the next field, the gingerbread man met a horse.

"You look yummy!" neighed the horse. "Stop, little man, I want to eat you!"

But the gingerbread man just ran faster. "I have run away from a little old woman, a little old man, a pig, and a cow, and I can run away from you!" he cried.

The horse started to gallop after the gingerbread man, but he was already halfway across the field. He turned and waved at the horse as he sang out:

**"Run, run, as fast as you can,
You can't catch me, I'm the gingerbread man!"**

The little old woman, the little old man, the pig, the cow, and the horse ran, but none of them could catch the little gingerbread man.

The little gingerbread man squeezed through a hedge and ran on, faster and faster, along a path through a shady wood. He grinned, feeling very pleased with himself, and rather proud of how fast he could run.

"No one can catch me!" he giggled.

But just a little farther on down the woodland path, the gingerbread man came to an abrupt stop. There before him flowed a wide river, completely blocking his way.

While the little gingerbread man was wondering how he was going to get across the river, a sly old fox came up to him.

"Hello, little man," said the fox, licking his lips. "You look like you could do with some help."

"Oh, yes please," cried the gingerbread man. "I've run away from a little old woman, a little old man, a pig, a cow, and a horse, and I need to get across this river so that I can keep on running. And I can't swim!"

"Well, jump on my back, and I'll carry you across the river," grinned the sly old fox. "You'll be safe and dry."

So the little gingerbread man climbed onto the fox's tail, and the fox began to swim across the river.

After a while, the fox said, "You're too heavy for my tail. Jump onto my back."

The little gingerbread man ran lightly down the fox's tail and jumped onto his back, clinging tightly onto his fur.

Soon, the fox said, "You're too heavy for my back. Jump onto my nose."

The little gingerbread man did as he was told and jumped onto the fox's nose.

At last, they reached the other side of the river. The gingerbread man was just about to jump to the ground when the hungry fox threw back his head. The little gingerbread man suddenly found himself tossed high in the air.

Then down fell the gingerbread man, and **SNAP!** went the mouth of the sly old fox.

And that was the end of the little gingerbread man!

The End

Goldilocks and the Three Bears

Once upon a time, there was a little girl named Goldilocks, who had beautiful golden hair. She lived in a pretty house right at the edge of the forest. Each morning she liked to play outside before breakfast, gathering flowers and looking at the animals who lived in the trees.

One day she strayed farther than usual. She skipped happily along the forest path, chasing butterflies, until she was far from home and very hungry.

Just as she was thinking that it would take a long time to walk back for breakfast, a delicious smell wafted through the woods. She followed it all the way to a little cottage.

"I wonder who lives here," Goldilocks said to herself. "Perhaps they would share their breakfast with me?" She knocked on the door, but there was no answer.

As Goldilocks pushed gently on the door, it swung open. The house inside was cozy and inviting. Even though she knew she shouldn't, Goldilocks stepped inside.

The delicious smell was coming from three bowls of steaming porridge on the table. There was a great big bowl, a middle-sized bowl, and a teeny-tiny bowl. Goldilocks was so hungry that—even though she knew she shouldn't—she tasted the porridge in the biggest bowl.

"Ew!" she cried. "This porridge is too hot!"

Next, she tasted the porridge in the middle-sized bowl. "Yuk!" she said. "This porridge is far too cold!"

So finally she tried the porridge in the teeny-tiny bowl.

"Yum!" Goldilocks said. "This porridge is just right!" And she ate it all up.

With her tummy nice and full, Goldilocks decided to rest before she set out for home. She looked around the room for somewhere to sit. There were three chairs—a great big chair, a middle-sized chair, and a teeny-tiny chair.

She climbed onto the great big chair.

"This chair is far too high," she said.

Next, she tried the middle-sized chair, but she sank deep into the cushions.

"No," she said, "this chair is far too squashy."

So she sat on the teeny-tiny chair.

"This chair is just right!" she said, settling down. But Goldilocks was very full of porridge, and too heavy for the teeny-tiny chair. It squeaked and creaked. It creaked and cracked. Then ...

Crash!

It broke into teeny-tiny pieces, and Goldilocks fell to the floor.

"Well, that wasn't a very good chair!" she said grumpily. Then, even though she knew she shouldn't, she went to look upstairs.

In the bedroom were three beds. A great big bed, a middle-sized bed, and a teeny-tiny bed.

She tried to lie down on the great big bed, but it wasn't at all comfy.

"This bed is too hard and lumpy," she grumbled. Then Goldilocks lay down on the middle-sized bed, but that was no better.

"This bed is too soft and squishy," she mumbled. And so at last she snuggled down in the teeny-tiny bed.

"This bed is just right!" she said, and fell fast asleep.

Now, whenever there is a house with porridge and chairs and beds, there is usually someone who lives there, and that was true of this house. Three big brown bears lived there: a great big daddy bear, a middle-sized mommy bear, and a teeny-tiny baby bear.

The three bears had made their porridge and gone out for a walk in the woods while it cooled down. At last, they went home for their breakfast.

"Why is the door open?" Daddy Bear said, in his deep, gruff voice.

"Why are there footprints on the floor?" Mommy Bear said, in her soft, low voice.

Baby Bear said nothing.

They went over to the table and Daddy Bear looked in his bowl.

"Someone's been eating my porridge!" he growled.

Mommy Bear looked in her bowl.

"Someone's been eating my porridge!" she exclaimed.

Baby Bear looked in his bowl.

"Someone's been eating my porridge—and they've eaten it all up!" he cried in his teeny-tiny voice.

Daddy Bear stomped over to his chair.

"Someone's been sitting in my chair!" he growled. "There's a long hair on it!"

"Someone's been sitting in my chair!" Mommy Bear exclaimed. "The cushions are all squashed!"

Baby Bear looked at his chair.

"Someone's been sitting in my chair," he cried, "and they've broken it into pieces!"

"Let's get to the bottom of this," Daddy Bear growled, and they padded upstairs to the bedroom.

Daddy Bear saw the rumpled covers of his bed.

"Someone's been sleeping in my bed!" he grumbled.

Mommy Bear saw the jumbled pillows on her bed.

"Someone's been sleeping in my bed!" she said.

Baby Bear padded up to his bed.

"Someone's been sleeping in my bed—and they're still there!" he cried.

The three bears crowded around the sleeping girl. Baby Bear reached out a fuzzy paw to touch her golden curls.

Goldilocks opened her eyes. Imagine her surprise when she saw three bears peering down at her! She leapt out of the bed, ran down the stairs, through the door, along the path, and all the way home. And she never visited the house of the three bears ever again.

The End

Puss in Boots

There was once an old miller who had three sons. When the miller died, he left the mill to his oldest son. The middle son was given the donkeys. The youngest son, a kind man who had always put his father and brothers before himself, was left nothing but his father's cat.

"What will become of me?" said the young miller's son with a sigh, looking at his cat.

"Buy me a fine pair of boots and I will help you make your fortune, for your father thought you deserved it," replied the cat.

A talking cat! The miller's son could not believe his ears.

So the miller's son bought the cat a fine pair of boots, and the two of them set off to seek their fortune.

After a while they came to a grand palace.

"Wouldn't it be wonderful to live so grandly," said the miller's son.

Later, while the miller's son was sleeping, the cat went hunting and caught a rabbit. He put it in a sack and took it to the palace.

"A gift to the king from my master, the Marquis of Carabas," said the cat, presenting it to the king.

The cat went back to the miller's son and told him what he had done.

"Now the king will want to know who the Marquis of Carabas is," laughed the cat.

A clever cat! The miller's son could not believe his ears.

Every day for a week, the cat delivered a gift to the king, each time saying it was from the Marquis of Carabas. After a while, the king became very curious and decided he'd like his daughter to meet this mysterious nobleman, whoever he might be.

When the cat heard that the king and his daughter were on their way, he wasted no time.

"You must take off all your clothes and stand in the river," the cat told his master.

The puzzled miller's son did as he was told, and the cat hid his master's tattered old clothes behind a rock.

When the cat heard the king's carriage approaching, he jumped onto the road and begged for help.

"Your gracious majesty," said the cat, "my master was robbed of all his clothes while he was bathing in the river."

The king gave the miller's son a suit of fine clothes to wear.

"Please join us in the carriage," said the king.

So the cat opened the door and the miller's son climbed in. He looked very handsome in his new suit. The king's daughter fell in love with him at once.

The cat ran ahead, cutting through the surrounding countryside. Every time he met people working in the fields, he told them, "If the king stops to ask who owns this land, you must tell him it belongs to the Marquis of Carabas."

Beyond the fields, the cat reached a grand castle. He spoke to the people working in a field next to it and discovered that it belonged to a fierce ogre. The cat stood bravely in his boots and knocked on the castle door.

"Who dares to disturb me?" roared a voice from inside the castle.

"I have heard that you are a very clever ogre," called the cat. "I have come to see what tricks you can do."

The ogre opened the door and immediately changed himself into a great snarling lion. The cat felt scared, but he didn't show it.

"That is quite a clever trick," said the cat, "but a lion is a very large creature. I think it would be a much better trick to change into something very small, like a mouse."

The ogre liked to show off his tricks. He changed at once into a little mouse. The cat pounced on the mouse and ate him up.

Then the cat went into the castle and told all of the servants that their new master was the Marquis of Carabas. They were glad to be rid of the fierce ogre, so they did not complain.

"The king is on his way to visit, and you must prepare a grand feast to welcome him," said the cat.

When the king's carriage arrived at the castle, the cat was waiting to welcome him.

"Your gracious majesty," he purred, "welcome to the home of my master, the Marquis of Carabas."

A cunning cat! The miller's son could not believe his eyes.

"You must ask for the princess's hand in marriage," whispered the cunning cat to his master.

The miller's son did as he was told.

The king, who was impressed by everything he saw, agreed.

Soon, the Marquis of Carabas and his wife were married, and they lived a very happy life together. The cat was made a lord of their court and was given the most splendid clothes, which he wore proudly along with those fine boots that the miller's son had bought him.

The End

Rumpelstiltskin

Once upon a time, there was a poor miller who had just one daughter. She was very beautiful, and he told many people about her.

One day, the king rode through the village. The miller desperately wanted to impress the king. "Your Highness, my daughter is very pretty and smart," he said.

But the king took no notice.

"She can also spin straw into gold!" the miller lied.

"Your daughter must be very clever. Bring her to the palace tomorrow so I can see for myself," demanded the king.

The miller didn't dare disobey the king, so the next day he brought his daughter to the palace. The king led the girl to a room filled with straw. On the floor stood a little stool and a spinning wheel.

"Spin this straw into gold by tomorrow morning, or you will be thrown into the dungeon," said the king. Then he left the room and locked the door.

The poor miller's daughter sat down on the stool and gazed at all the straw around her. She wept bitterly at the impossible task before her.

All of a sudden, the door sprang open, and in came the strangest little man she had ever seen.

"Why are you crying?" he asked.

"I have to spin all this straw into gold before the morning, but I don't know how," replied the girl sadly.

"If you give me your pretty necklace, I will spin the straw into gold," said the strange little man.

"Oh, thank you!" gasped the girl, wiping away her tears and handing over her necklace.

The little man sat down in front of the spinning wheel and set to work.

All night long, the little man spun, and by morning the room was filled with reels of gold. And just as suddenly as he had appeared, the strange man disappeared.

When the king arrived, he was astonished to see so much gold.

"You have done very well," he said, "but I wonder if you can do the same thing again?"

He took the miller's daughter to a much bigger room. It, too, was filled with straw.

"Spin this straw into gold by tomorrow morning, or you will be thrown into the dungeon," said the king, and once more he locked the girl in the room.

The miller's daughter was very frightened. The strange little man appeared before her again.

"Don't cry," he said. "Give me your shiny ring, and I will spin the straw into gold."

She handed over her ring gratefully, and the little man set to work. Once again, all the straw was turned into gold.

The king wanted to try one more time.

"If you can do this again, you shall be my queen!" cried the king.

The poor miller's daughter wept even more bitterly this time when the king left.

"Why are you crying?" said the little man, appearing for the third time. "You know that I will help you."

"But I have nothing left to give you," sobbed the girl.

"If you become queen," replied the little man, "you can give me your first-born child."

The desperate miller's daughter agreed to the man's request. And once again, he spun all the straw into gold.

The king was so delighted when he saw all the gold the next day that he kept his promise and married the miller's daughter.

The new queen was very happy and soon forgot about the promise she had made to the strange little man who saved her from the dungeon.

A year later, the king and queen had a beautiful baby boy.

Late one night, the little man appeared in the queen's bedroom as she watched over her sleeping baby.

"I'm here for your baby," he said. "Just as you promised."

The queen was horrified. "Oh, please, take all my jewels and money instead," she begged. "Not my son!"

"No," replied the little man. "You made a promise. But I will give you three days. If in that time you can guess my name, then you will keep your baby."

The desperate queen agreed. The next day she sent messengers all over the kingdom to collect all the boys' names they could find.

That night, the strange man appeared again, and the queen read out the names she had gathered. But after each name he just laughed.

The next day, the queen sent her messengers out to find even more names, and that night she read out the new names when the little man appeared. But once again, the queen's guesses were wrong.

On the third day, the poor queen was in despair. It was getting late by the time her last messenger returned.

"Your Highness, I haven't found any new names," he said, "but as I was returning through the forest, I saw a little man leaping and dancing around a fire, singing a song. It went like this:

'The queen will never win my game,
For Rumpelstiltskin is my name!'"

The queen was overjoyed!

When the little man appeared that night, the queen said, "Are you perhaps called ... Rumpelstiltskin?"

The little man was furious. He stamped his foot so hard it went through the floor. Then, pulling on his leg until he was free, he stomped out of the room and was never seen or heard from again.

And the king and queen, and their son, lived happily ever after.

The End

Beauty and the Beast

There was once a rich merchant who had three daughters. The youngest daughter had a kind heart, unlike her jealous sisters. She was called Beauty.

Everything changed one winter when the merchant lost all his money and was forced to move into a little cottage. The two elder daughters wept in anger, fearing no one would marry them now. They would stay in bed all day while Beauty rose at four each morning and cleaned the cottage and cooked their meals.

One day, the merchant received good news. One of his ships had been found, which meant he would have money again. He immediately set off for town.

"Bring me back a velvet cape," demanded the eldest sister.

"And I'll have a silk gown," added the second sister.

"What about you, Beauty?" asked her father kindly.

"Please bring me a rose, Father," said Beauty politely.

Beauty worried terribly about her father and longed for his safe return, but she knew her sisters would tease her mercilessly if she said this.

Sadly, the merchant had been given the wrong information. It was not his ship that had been found after all. With a heavy heart, he rode back, failing to notice the snow falling so thickly. Soon he was lost. He wandered for hours, and when night fell, he began to despair. At last he spotted a golden light coming from a great castle.

Pushing on the open door, he found himself inside a dining hall where a fire blazed and a table was laid for one person. But there was no one to greet him. At last he said to himself, "I can wait no longer. Surely the kind master will pardon me if I eat alone."

After a good night's sleep, the merchant set off. Wending his way through a scented rose garden, he was reminded of Beauty's request. As he broke off a single red rose, there was a thunderous roar and a hideous creature appeared before him.

"So this is how you repay my kindness!" snarled the creature. "I saved your life but you choose to steal the thing I love most. You deserve to die."

"Forgive me, Lord," begged the merchant. "I only wanted to pluck a rose for my youngest daughter."

"Call me Beast," snapped the creature. "I will spare your life if one of your daughters comes to stay with me of her own free will. But if none of them agrees, you must return within three months."

With a sad heart, the merchant agreed.

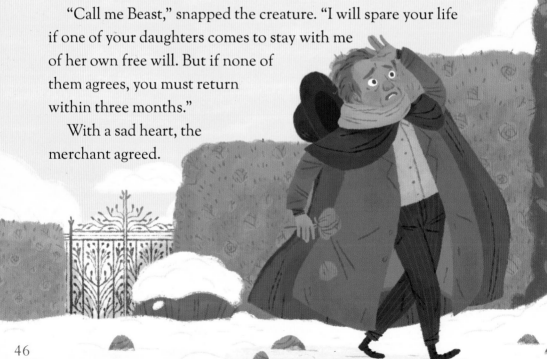

On hearing her
father's story, Beauty persuaded
him to take her to the Beast's castle.

When she arrived, she could hardly dare look at the creature.
But Beauty very soon came to realize that he had a good heart.

One evening as he joined her for supper, the Beast asked her,
"Do you find me ugly?"

And for the first time Beauty looked at his face.

"Yes, but you are very kind," she replied honestly.

The Beast seemed pleased by her answer and suddenly asked if
she would be his wife.

"No, Beast," she replied simply. And the Beast let out a
painful cry.

As the time passed, Beauty came to enjoy her life at the castle. She had everything she needed. As a sign of his love for her, the Beast gave Beauty a magic mirror to show her what was happening at home.

One day as she looked into the mirror, she saw her father was ill.

"I must go to my father," she told the Beast. "If you let me leave, I promise I will return."

Heartened by these words, the Beast agreed. "Take your mirror with you," he said. "And remember, if you do not return in one week, I shall die of grief."

Beauty's father was overjoyed to see her, and he soon became well again. The foolish sisters had both married, but were unhappy. So they tricked Beauty into staying longer than the week. One day when Beauty was looking in her magic mirror, she saw the Beast was ill. She knew she had to return.

Arriving back at the castle, she found him close to death.

"You broke your promise," the Beast whispered, "and now I must die."

"No! No!" cried Beauty in anguish. And at that moment she knew she loved him.

"I want to be your wife," she pleaded. And as her tears fell on the Beast's face, a bright light dazzled her. Suddenly, standing before her was the most handsome man she had ever set eyes on.

"Where is the Beast?" she cried.

"I was your Beast," smiled the young man. "By choosing to stay with me and promising to be my wife, you have broken the spell."

Beauty and her Prince were soon married and lived happily in their castle.

The End

The Tortoise and the Hare

The hare and the tortoise were neighbors. Hare was always in a hurry, rushing from one important task to another. He was so fast and busy that sometimes he could barely remember where he was going. Tortoise, on the other hand, plodded steadily along. He didn't go to many different places in a day, but he always got to where he needed to be.

One day, Tortoise was walking slowly along the road when Hare sped past him. Hare looked over his shoulder and called out, "Hurry up, Tortoise—you'll never get there!"

"I will," Tortoise said calmly, "I will. Slow, but steady."

Hare turned back and ran around Tortoise three times, laughing. Then he ran on.

Half an hour later, Hare came back. Tortoise was still going in the same direction, and he hadn't gotten very far. Hare laughed.

"You're so slow!" he said. "How do you ever get anywhere?"

"Look," Tortoise said. "One step at a time. One foot after the other. Slow, but steady."

"You're hopeless!" Hare said. "It will take you all day just to get to the end of the road!"

At last, Tortoise was too cross to ignore Hare any longer.

"I get everywhere I want to go!" he said. "And if you don't believe me, I'll challenge you to a race. You can pick the route, the day, and the time."

Hare laughed until he fell over. He rolled around on the floor, tears running along his whiskers.

"A race?" he gasped. "Between you and me? That's ridiculous! You don't stand a chance."

"Are you scared?" Tortoise asked. "Because if not, let's do it."

Hare could hardly stop laughing, but they arranged the race for the next day and asked Fox to judge it. They would start from an old oak tree and race all the way to the river.

Tortoise set out early that evening so that he would be at the start line on time in the morning.

Hare went home for a long sleep and got up late. He ran to the oak tree and found Tortoise ready and waiting. All the other animals had come out to watch.

"Fox is waiting for you at the river," Bear said. "We can start whenever you're ready."

Hare and Tortoise got into position.

"On your marks," said Tortoise.

"Get set," said Hare.

"Go!" shouted all the animals.

Start

And off went the tortoise and the hare.

Hare sprinted ahead, bounding along the path. Tortoise lifted one foot, and put it down. Then he lifted the other foot, and put it down. Slowly, slowly. By the time Tortoise reached the first bush, Hare was a tiny spot in the distance. By the time he reached the second bush, Hare was nowhere to be seen.

After a few minutes, Hare could see the river ahead. He paused and looked around. He couldn't see Tortoise at all.

"He is so slow!" he laughed to himself. "He won't be here for hours. I might as well have a rest." So Hare sat down under a tree not far from the finish line. The sun was warm, and the lazy buzz of bees visiting the flowers around him was soothing. Soon Hare dozed off.

Back along the path, Tortoise kept on, slow but steady, one step at a time, one foot after the other.

After an hour, Hare woke up and peered into the distance. He could just see Tortoise coming toward him, slow but steady, and still far away.

"He's so slow!" Hare said to himself. "He won't be here for hours. I might as well go back to sleep." And that's just what he did.

Tortoise kept on, slow but steady, his heavy shell wobbling along the path. Hare slept on in the hot sun.

When Hare woke up, he couldn't see Tortoise anywhere.

Finish

"Where has he gone?" he said. "He won't be here for hours, I'm sure. I could just go back to sleep." But it was late afternoon and the sun was low in the sky. "I'm sick of this race," he said to himself. "I should finish so I can go home and nap in my own bed." And he sprang up and ran as fast as he could to the finish line.

Tortoise was waiting for him by the river.

"Where have you been?" asked Tortoise. "I've been here for hours. You are so slow!"

Hare tried to explain, but neither Tortoise nor Fox would listen.

"But I'm faster!" Hare complained. "It's not fair!"

"The rules were simple," Fox said. "Tortoise won."

"The race was to get here first," Tortoise smiled, "not to run fastest. Slow and steady wins the race!" And slowly, steadily, he turned around to begin his journey home.

The End

Snow White and the Seven Dwarves

Once there was a queen who longed for a daughter. As she sat sewing by her window one winter's day, she pricked her finger on the needle. Three drops of blood fell from her finger, and she thought, "I wish I could have a daughter with lips as red as blood, hair as black as the ebony of this window-frame, and skin as white as the snow outside."

Before long she gave birth to a beautiful baby daughter with blood-red lips, ebony hair, and skin as white as snow.

"I will call you Snow White," whispered the queen to her new baby.

But soon after, the queen died and the king married again. His new bride was very beautiful, but also very vain. She had a magic mirror, and every day she would look into it and ask:

**"Mirror, mirror, on the wall,
Who is the fairest of them all?"**

And the mirror would reply:

> **"You, O Queen,**
> **are the fairest of them all."**

As Snow White became more
beautiful with every day that passed,
her stepmother became more and more
jealous. One day she asked the mirror:

> **"Mirror, mirror, on the wall,**
> **Who is the fairest of them all?"**

And the mirror replied:

> **"You, O Queen, are fair, it's true,**
> **But young Snow White**
> **is fairer than you."**

When the queen heard these words she was furious.
She called for her huntsman.

"Take Snow White into the forest and kill her!" she commanded.

The huntsman had to obey his queen. He led the beautiful girl
deep into the forest. When he pulled out his knife, Snow White
was very afraid and started to cry.

"Please, don't hurt me," she begged.

The huntsman took pity on her and decided to let her go.

"You must run as far from here as you can," he told her.

Snow White fled into the forest.

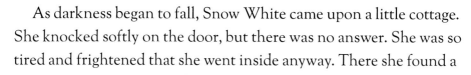

As darkness began to fall, Snow White came upon a little cottage. She knocked softly on the door, but there was no answer. She was so tired and frightened that she went inside anyway. There she found a table laid with seven places and a bedroom with seven little beds. Snow White lay down on the seventh bed and fell fast asleep.

She awoke to find seven little men all staring at her in amazement.

"Who are you?" she asked.

"We are the seven dwarves who live here," said one of the little men. "We work in the mines all day. Who are you?"

"I am Snow White," she replied.

When she told the dwarves her story, they were horrified.

"You can stay here with us," said the eldest dwarf.

So every day, the seven dwarves went off to work, and Snow White stayed at the cottage and cooked and cleaned for them.

"Do not open the door to anyone," they told her as they left each morning, worried that the wicked queen would try to find her.

Meanwhile, the wicked queen asked her mirror:

> "Mirror, mirror, on the wall,
> Who is the fairest of them all?"

And the mirror replied:

> "You, O Queen, are fair, it's true,
> But Snow White is still fairer than you.
> Deep in the forest with seven little men,
> Snow White is living in a cozy den."

The wicked queen was furious and vowed that she would kill Snow White herself. She added poison to a juicy apple, then disguised herself as a peddler woman and set off into the forest.

"Who will buy my fresh apples?" the wicked queen called out as she knocked at the door of the dwarves' cottage. Snow White loved apples, but remembered that she must not open the door to anyone. Instead, she opened the window to take a look. When the peddler woman offered her an apple, she was nervous.

"There's no need to be frightened," said the disguised queen. She placed the apple in Snow White's hand. Snow White hesitated, then took a bite. The poison worked the moment it touched Snow White's beautiful red lips. The piece of apple became stuck in her throat, and she fell down to the ground.

When the seven dwarves returned that evening, they were heartbroken to find that their beloved Snow White was dead. Such was their grief that they could not bear to bury her. The dwarves made a glass coffin for Snow White and placed it in the forest, where they took turns watching over it.

One day, a prince rode by.

"Who is this beautiful girl?" asked the prince.

The dwarves told the prince Snow White's sad story, and the prince wept.

"Please let me take her away," begged the prince. "I promise I will watch over her."

The dwarves could see how much the prince loved Snow White, so they agreed to let her go.

As the prince's servants lifted the coffin, they lost their grip. The fall jolted the piece of poisoned apple from Snow White's throat, and she came back to life.

When Snow White saw the handsome
prince, she fell deeply in love with him.
"Will you marry me?" asked the prince.
Snow White happily agreed.
Before long, the couple were married. The
dwarves joined them in the prince's castle, and they
all lived happily together for the rest of their lives.

The End

The Three Little Pigs

Once upon a time, three little pigs lived together with their mother. As they grew bigger, their small house became too crowded. So at last she sent them off into the world to seek their fortunes.

"Be careful," she said. "Here, you are safe from the big, bad wolf. But out there, you will need to build strong houses."

The pigs set off happily. After a short time, the first little pig met a farmer pulling a cartload of straw.

"Please may I have some straw to build a house?" the little pig asked.

"Certainly," the farmer said, "but it won't make a very strong house."

The little pig didn't listen. He took the bundles of straw and stacked them up to make a house. When it was finished, he went inside for a rest.

Soon, the big, bad wolf came down the road. He hadn't eaten all day. When he saw the new house of straw, his tummy rumbled and he licked his lips.

"I smell piggy," he said to himself. "Yum!"

He peeked in through the window.

"Little pig, little pig, let me come in," he growled.

"No way!" the pig shouted. "Not by the hairs on my chinny-chin-chin!"

"Well, this house doesn't look very strong," the wolf said.

"I'll huff and I'll puff, and I'll blow your house down!"

So he huffed and he puffed, and he blew the house down. Straw flew everywhere, and the little pig ran away as fast as he could.

The second little pig walked a little farther. At last he came across a woodcutter with a pile of sticks.

"Please could I have some sticks to build a house?" the little pig asked.

"Certainly," said the woodcutter. "Take as many as you like, but they won't make a very strong house."

The second little pig didn't listen. He picked up all the sticks he could carry and took them to a clearing. He piled them up to make a cozy house. When it was finished, he went inside and settled down with a cup of tea.

The big, bad wolf was cross and hungry. When he saw the house of sticks, his tummy grumbled and he licked his lips.

"I smell piggy," he said to himself. "Yum, yum!"

He pushed his nose against the door.

"Little pig, little pig, let me come in," he growled.

"No way!" the second little pig shouted. "Not by the hairs on my chinny-chin-chin!"

"Well, this house doesn't look very strong," the wolf said.

"I'll huff and I'll puff, and I'll blow your house down!"

And so he huffed and he puffed, and he blew the house down. The sticks tumbled to the ground, and the little pig ran away as fast as he could.

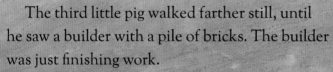

The third little pig walked farther still, until
he saw a builder with a pile of bricks. The builder
was just finishing work.

"Please could I have some bricks to build a little house?"
the third little pig asked.

"Certainly," the builder said. "Those are left over. Take
as many as you want."

So the third little pig carried the bricks away and built
a beautiful house. When he had finished, he went inside, put
a pot of water on the fire and started to make some soup.

After a while, his two brothers came running up the path.

"Let us in!" they shouted. "There's a big, bad wolf coming!"

The third little pig quickly let them in. They locked and
bolted the door and sat down to wait.

Before long, the big, bad wolf came huffing and puffing up the path. When he saw the new brick house, his tummy rumbled and grumbled and he licked his lips.

"I smell piggy—and soup!" he said to himself. "Yum, yum, yum!"

He knocked hard on the door.

"Little pig, little pig, let me come in!" he roared.

"No way!" the third little pig shouted.

"Not by the hairs on my chinny-chin-chin!"

"Well, then," the wolf said,

"I'll huff and I'll puff,

and I'll blow your house down!"

And so he huffed and he puffed, and he huffed and he puffed ... but the house stood firm.

The wolf looked up and saw the chimney. He climbed onto the roof, and down the chimney he went—straight into the pot of hot soup.

"Owwwooooooo!"

He jumped out of the pot and ran yowling and howling out into the cool night. The big, bad wolf ran up the path, over the hills and far away, never to be seen again. The three little pigs lived happily ever after, all together in the strong brick house.

The End

How the Rhinoceros Got His Skin

Long ago, among the tall trees near the shores of the Red Sea, lived a very rude rhinoceros. He had no manners then, and he has no manners now. You could recognize him by the horn on his nose, but in those days his skin was smooth and tight, and there wasn't a wrinkle in sight! He had three buttons on his tummy, which made it look just like a well-fitted jacket.

One day as Rhinoceros was searching for food, a traveler arrived on the beach and decided to bake a cake in his little oven. He sang to himself as he mixed flour and water, and currants and plums and lots of sugar. Happy with his mixture, he popped it in the oven while he dozed under the burning sun. Soon the sweet smell of cake filled the air.

"Delicious!" smiled the traveler when the cake was ready.

In the nearby woods, Rhinoceros suddenly stopped in his tracks and lifted his head. He sniffed and sniffed.

"Cake!" he snorted as the warm smells wafted above his horn. Then he followed his nose and headed for the beach. When the polite traveler saw him coming he said, "Good morning," but the rude creature didn't even give a grunt.

Instead, he charged ahead, knocking the cake out of the traveler's hands. Then he spiked the cake with his horn, and lumbered back to his home. There he lay in the shade enjoying every crumb.

Meanwhile, the traveler climbed a palm tree and sat on high, thinking and planning.

"Just wait," he muttered, "I'll teach that rhino a lesson."

A few weeks later, when searing heat prompted everyone to take to the sea, the traveler knew the time had come. He was sitting on the beach wearing his hat to screen him from the ferocious sun when he spied Rhinoceros. His eyes followed the creature as he heaved his great body along the sand. Not noticing the traveler, Rhinoceros finally stopped.

Rhinoceros slowly undid his three buttons, took off his skin, and carried it over his shoulder as he went down to the sea to bathe. Leaving his skin at the edge of the water, he waddled into the sea. The traveler immediately jumped up. He danced around the skin and rubbed his hands with glee.

"I'm ready!" the traveler cried. "Just you wait and see." Then he set off back to his camp.

As the traveler only ever ate cake, and rarely cleaned up, there were plenty of crumbs around his camp.

"Lots of crumbs! Crumbly crumbs!" he sang as he quickly filled his hat with the stale cake crumbs. Then he raced back to the beach.

Picking up the skin of the rhinoceros, the traveler sprinkled the inside with lots of dry, tickly cake and some baked currants. Then he left the skin for Rhinoceros, climbed to the top of his palm tree, and waited.

Rhinoceros took his time in the sea. He lay on his back and blew bubbles through his nose. He splashed and splashed, never caring about others in the water. Finally, as his great big tummy started to rumble, and feeling much cooler from his swim, Rhinoceros returned to the beach.

Thinking about what he was going to eat, Rhinoceros picked up his skin and buttoned it up. No sooner had he finished closing the last button than the crumbs started to itch. He wriggled and wriggled. He began to scratch, but that made it worse.

"Ow! Ow!" he cried loudly.

Then he lay down on the sand and rolled and rolled and rolled, but every time he rolled, the cake crumbs dug into him, making it more and more uncomfortable. He was beginning to feel very hot again and very, very crabby.

He lumbered up to a palm tree and rubbed himself against the trunk but still the itching continued. He pressed his shoulders so hard against the tree that he rubbed his skin into a great fold. Then his legs started to itch so he rubbed them up and down the tree until folds appeared over both legs. He was now feeling very tired and as he pressed his itchy tummy against the tree, he rubbed off every button. Finally, a huge fold of skin appeared across his tummy.

The traveler looked down from the palm tree, watching his plan working. The rhinoceros became more and more bad-tempered as the cake crumbs continued to itch and scratch.

Feeling exhausted and very angry, Rhinoceros finally gave up and headed back home.

And from that day to this, every rhinoceros has great folds in his skin and a very bad temper, all because of the cake crumbs inside.

The End

The Elves and the Shoemaker

There was once a shoemaker who lived with his wife. Although they worked from dawn until dusk, they were very poor.

"We have only enough leather to make one more pair of shoes to sell," the shoemaker told his wife one day.

"What will become of us?" asked the shoemaker's wife. "How can we live without money?"

The shoemaker shook his head sadly. He cut out the leather and left it on his workbench, ready to start work the next morning.

Then the couple went to bed with heavy hearts.

In the middle of the night, when the house was quiet and pale moonlight shone into the workshop, two elves appeared. They were dressed in rags but had eyes as bright as buttons. They explored the workshop, balancing on cotton reels and peering into cupboards. Soon they found the leather.

Elves are busy little creatures, and so they set to work at once, snipping and sewing. As they worked, they sang:

> "Busy little elves are we,
> Working by the pale moonlight.
> While the humans are asleep,
> We are busy through the night!"

By dawn, the two little elves had finished their work and disappeared.

When the shoemaker came to start work the next morning, he could not believe his eyes. There, on his workbench, was the finest pair of shoes he had ever seen.

"The stitches are so delicate," he said, as he showed his astonished wife the beautiful shoes. "I will place them in my window for everyone to see."

Soon, a rich gentleman walked by the shop. He saw the stylish shoes and came inside.

The rich gentleman tried on the shoes, and they fit perfectly. He was so delighted that he gave the shoemaker twice the asking price.

"I can buy more leather!" said the shoemaker happily to his wife.

That evening, the shoemaker cut out the leather for two more pairs of shoes. He left it on his workbench for the next morning.

In the middle of the night, the two elves appeared again. They explored the workshop, climbing on the tools and swinging from shoelaces. Soon they found the leather.

The elves set to work at once, snipping and sewing. As they worked, they sang:

> "Busy little elves are we,
> Working by the pale moonlight.
> While the humans are asleep,
> We are busy through the night!"

By dawn, the two little elves had finished their work and disappeared.

Once again the shoemaker came into his workshop and found the shoes, neatly finished on his bench. The shoemaker placed them in his window.

By now, the rich gentleman had told his friends about the shoemaker's fine work. The two pairs of shoes sold that same day for more money than the shoemaker could ever have dreamed of. The shoemaker now had enough money to buy leather to make four new pairs of shoes.

"But who can be helping us?" asked the shoemaker's wife.

That evening, the shoemaker cut out the leather for four more pairs of shoes. He left it on his workbench as usual. Then, the shoemaker and his wife hid and waited.

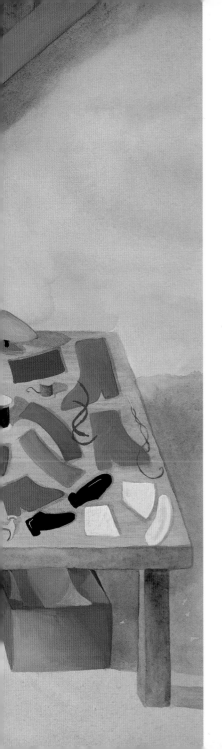

In the middle of the night, they watched in amazement as the two little elves appeared. As usual, the elves explored the workshop. They danced with colorful ribbons and juggled pretty beads. Soon they found the leather. Again, the elves set to work, snipping and sewing. As they worked, they sang:

"Busy little elves are we,
Working by the pale moonlight.
While the humans are asleep,
We are busy through the night!"

By dawn, the two little elves had finished their work and disappeared.

"We must repay our little helpers for their kindness," said the shoemaker to his wife.

The couple thought hard about what they could do to thank the elves.

"They were dressed in rags," said the shoemaker's wife. "Why don't we make them some fine new clothes?"

Although they were now very busy in their shop, the shoemaker and his wife spent every spare moment they had making their gift for the elves. They cut out fine cloth and leather, and sewed tiny seams. Soon they had made two little pairs of trousers, two smart coats, two sturdy pairs of boots, and two warm, woolly scarves. They placed the little outfits on the workbench for the elves to find.

That night, when the house was quiet and pale moonlight shone into the workshop, the shoemaker and his wife hid and waited. They watched happily as the two little elves appeared. As usual, the elves explored the workshop. They made a tightrope from thread and bounced on a pincushion. Soon they found the tiny little outfits. They were delighted! They put on the trousers, the coats, the boots and the scarves and danced merrily around the workbench.

As they danced, they sang:

> "Handsome little elves are we,
> Dancing by the pale moonlight.
> While the humans are asleep,
> We make merry through the night!"

And then, the smart little elves put on their hats and disappeared. The shoemaker and his wife never saw the little elves again. But the couple continued to make fine shoes for their shop, and from that day on they always prospered.

The End

Hansel and Gretel

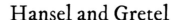

Once upon a time, there were two children named Hansel and Gretel. They lived in a small cottage at the edge of the forest with their father and stepmother.

Hansel and Gretel's father was a woodcutter. He was very poor, and the family didn't have much food to eat.

The day came when there was hardly any food left at all.

"What are we to do?" cried the father.

The stepmother, who didn't like Hansel and Gretel, said, "We must take the children into the thickest part of the forest and leave them there. There are just too many mouths to feed."

"We can't do that!" protested the father, for he loved his children dearly.

"We must or we'll all die of hunger!" screeched his wife. "The children are going, and that is that."

From their bedroom, Hansel and Gretel overheard the conversation. Gretel burst into tears.

"Don't worry," Hansel said. "I'll look after you."

When their parents went to bed, Hansel crept out of the house. All around lay little white pebbles that shone like coins in the silvery moonlight. He filled his pockets with them and then went back to bed.

Early the next morning, the stepmother hurried Hansel and Gretel out of bed.

"Come on, children. We're going into the forest to chop wood," she told them.

With a heavy heart, the woodcutter led his children into the forest. As they walked along, Hansel dropped the pebbles from his pockets onto the path.

When they reached the middle of the forest, the woodcutter said, "Wait here. We'll be back as soon as we've finished chopping wood."

Hansel and Gretel waited all day, but their father and stepmother didn't come back. Soon, it was dark among the thick trees. Gretel was frightened.

"We'll find our way home," Hansel comforted his sister.

When the moon rose high in the sky, the white pebbles that Hansel had left on the path lit up. He grabbed his sister's hand.

"Come on, Gretel, the pebbles will show us the way home!"

When Hansel and Gretel returned, the woodcutter was relieved to see his children again, but their stepmother was furious.

Before long the woodcutter and his family had very little food again.

"Tomorrow we will take the children deeper into the forest. They must not find their way home!" the stepmother cried.

This time, as they were led deep into the forest, Hansel left a trail of breadcrumbs.

When their parents didn't return from chopping wood, Hansel said, "We'll follow the breadcrumbs I dropped on the path. They will lead us home."

But when the moon came up, Hansel and Gretel couldn't see any crumbs. "The birds must have eaten them all!" whispered Hansel.

Frightened and hungry, Hansel and Gretel curled up under a tree and went to sleep, waiting anxiously for daylight.

The next morning, they wandered through the forest. After a while they came to a clearing and a little cottage.

"Hansel, look!" cried Gretel. "That cottage is made out of sweets and gingerbread!"

The children were so hungry they grabbed some sweets from the walls of the house. Just then, the door opened and an old woman hobbled out.

"Come in, children," she said, smiling. "I've got plenty more food in here."

Their stomachs growling, Hansel and Gretel followed the old woman into the cottage. After a delicious meal, she showed them to two little beds and they lay down to sleep.

The children didn't know that the old woman was actually a wicked old witch who liked to eat children!

When Hansel and Gretel woke up from their nap, the witch grabbed Hansel and locked him in a cage. She set Gretel to work cleaning and cooking huge meals to fatten up Hansel.

Weeks passed. Every morning the witch went up to the cage.

"Hold out your finger, boy. I want to feel if you are fat enough to eat."

Hansel, being a smart boy, would hold out an old chicken bone instead. The witch's eyesight was so bad that she thought the bone was Hansel's finger. She wondered why the boy wasn't getting any fatter.

One day, the witch grew impatient.

"I can't wait any longer," she screeched. "I'm going to cook Hansel now!"

Gretel was terrified.

"We'll bake some bread to eat with your brother," said the witch. "Go and check if the oven is hot enough."

Grabbing Gretel's arm, the wicked witch pushed her roughly toward the open oven door. Grinning horribly, she licked her cracked lips. She was planning on eating Gretel too, and couldn't wait for her delicious meal!

Gretel guessed the witch's trick. "I'm too big to fit in there," she said.

"Oh, you silly girl," cackled the witch. "Even I can fit in there." And she put her head into the oven to prove she was right. Gretel gave her a giant push and the witch fell right inside. Gretel quickly slammed the oven door shut.

"Hansel, the witch is dead!" cried Gretel as she unlocked her brother's cage.

As Hansel and Gretel made their way out of the house, they discovered that it was full of sparkling jewels and gold coins. The children stuffed their pockets with treasure.

"Come on, Gretel," laughed Hansel. "Let's go home!"

Their father was overjoyed to see them. He told them that their stepmother had died while they were gone and they had nothing to fear any more. Hansel and Gretel showed their father the jewels and coins. They would be poor no longer!

And from then on, the woodcutter and his children were never hungry again.

The End

The Dog and His Reflection

Puppy was having the best day of his life. The farmer had just given him his very first bone. It was a magnificent bone, with lots of juicy meat. Although Puppy couldn't wait to eat, he wanted to show it off around the farm first.

"What a fine bone," said Hen as Puppy strutted proudly past.

"It's nearly as big as you!" laughed Cow.

"Mmm, that looks tasty," said Fox. "You wouldn't like to share it, would you?"

Puppy quickly trotted off, the bone still clenched firmly in his teeth. He was looking for a place where he could be on his own, with no one else hungrily watching him. So he headed for the woods.

Puppy had never been into the woods before. It always looked very dark and scary, but it seemed a good place to enjoy his bone in peace. But the woods was even scarier than he imagined. An owl hooted at him from the trees.

"Sorry, didn't mean to frighten you," said the owl. "I was just admiring your fine bone. Make sure you take good care of it."

Although the owl turned out to be friendly, Puppy still didn't really like the woods. So, he ran all the way through to the other side, where he found lush green fields.

Puppy had never been this far away from home. It was exciting but a little scary, too. Soon he came to a wooden bridge over a very clear river. This was very different from the streams around the farm, which were all muddy and full of weeds. Puppy was curious.

On the other side of the bridge, a family of rabbits were playing in the field.

"The rabbits won't want to share my bone," Puppy thought. "I'll dash over the river and dig into it in peace."

By now Puppy was feeling very hungry indeed. All he wanted was to sit in the soft grass and chew his bone in peace. He wobbled as he started crossing the old bridge. He tried not to look down, but when he reached the middle, he could not resist a quick glance.

He was surprised to see another dog peeping out from
under the bridge.

Puppy went a bit closer to the edge to have a better look. As
he did so, the other dog peeped out even farther so Puppy could now
see his whole face. In between his teeth, he was also carrying a bone!
And it looked just as big and juicy as Puppy's bone.

"I wish I could have that bone too," thought Puppy.

So, he started to growl at the other dog, hoping that it would make
him drop the bone and run away.

Now the owl had flown out of the woods and come to perch
on a nearby tree. He was watching Puppy very carefully.

"Oh dear," said the owl with a shake of his head.

Puppy began to growl even louder at the other dog. After all, that dog did not look any bigger than himself. But the other dog still refused to run off, seeming to growl back.

"It's not a real dog or a real bone," hooted the owl. "Be happy with what you already have instead of being greedy and trying to have even more."

But Puppy was not listening. He suddenly let out the fiercest bark he had ever made. **"Woof! Woof!"**

Immediately, the other dog dropped his bone.

Puppy felt very proud of himself. But then he realized that he didn't have his own bone either. It must have fallen out when he opened his mouth to bark. Yes, there it was—right at the bottom of the river!

Puppy sniffed miserably. He noticed that the other dog was sniffing miserably too.

It was then that Puppy finally realized that the other dog wasn't real at all. Nor was the bone. The owl was right. It was just himself, reflected in the clear water.

Seeing what had happened, one of the little rabbits
hopped on to the bridge.

"Don't worry," he cried. "Come and play with us."

But Puppy did not feel like playing. Instead, feeling
hungry and sad, he set off on his own.

Just as the wise owl had told him, he should have been
content with the gift he had and not greedily wanted
even more.

The End

Rapunzel

Once upon a time, a young couple lived in a cottage beside a stone wall. They were very poor, but very happy as the woman was expecting a baby. On the other side of the wall lived an old witch. The witch grew many herbs and vegetables in her garden, but she kept them all for herself.

One day the couple had only a few potatoes to eat for their supper. They thought of the wonderful vegetable patch on the other side of the wall. It was full of delicious-looking carrots, cabbages, and tomatoes.

"Surely it wouldn't matter if we took just a few vegetables," said the wife, gazing longingly over the wall.

"We could make such good soup," agreed her husband.

So the young man quickly climbed over the wall and started to fill his basket with vegetables.

Suddenly he heard an angry voice.

"How dare you steal my vegetables!" It was the witch.

"Please don't hurt me," begged the young man. "My wife is going to have a baby soon!"

"You may keep the vegetables—and your life," she croaked. "But you must give me the baby when it is born." Terrified, the man had to agree.

Months later, the woman gave birth to a little girl. Immediately, the witch arrived and grabbed the child. Though the parents begged and cried, the cruel witch took the baby. She named her Rapunzel.

Years passed, and Rapunzel grew up to be kind and beautiful. The witch was so afraid of losing her that she built a tall tower with no door and only one window. She planted thorn bushes all around it, then she locked Rapunzel in the tower and never let her see anyone else.

Each day, Rapunzel brushed and combed her long, golden locks. And each day the witch came to visit her, standing at the foot of the tower and calling out, "Rapunzel, Rapunzel, let down your hair." Rapunzel hung her hair out of the window, and the witch climbed up it to sit and talk with her. But Rapunzel was very lonely. She longed to leave the tower and make friends her own age. Each day, she sat at her window and sang sadly.

One day, a young prince rode by and heard beautiful singing coming from the witch's garden. He hid behind a thorn bush, hoping to see the singer. But instead he saw the witch. He watched as she stood below the tower and called, "Rapunzel, Rapunzel, let down your hair."

The prince saw the cascade of golden hair fall from the window, and he watched the witch climb up it.

He waited until the witch climbed back down the hair and returned to her house. Rapunzel began her song again.

Enchanted by Rapunzel's lovely voice, the prince climbed over the wall and crept to the tower.

"Rapunzel, Rapunzel, let down your hair," he called softly.

Rapunzel let down her locks and the prince climbed up.

Poor Rapunzel was terribly afraid—she had never seen anyone except the witch before. When the prince explained that he only wanted to be her friend, Rapunzel was delighted. From then on, the prince came to visit her every day. Each time, he carefully waited until after the witch's visit before calling to Rapunzel to let down her hair.

Months passed, and Rapunzel and the prince fell in love.

"How can we be together?" Rapunzel cried. "The witch will never let me go."

The prince had an idea. He brought silk, which Rapunzel knotted together to make a ladder so that she could escape from the tower.

One day, without thinking, Rapunzel remarked to the witch, "It's much harder to pull you up than the prince!"

The witch was furious!

"Prince?" she shouted. "What prince?"

The witch grabbed Rapunzel's long hair and cut it off. Then she used her magic to send Rapunzel far into the forest. The girl made her home among the animals and birds, and sang sadly as she collected fruit and berries to eat.

Soon, the prince came to the tower and called,

"Rapunzel, Rapunzel, let down your hair."

The witch held the golden hair out of the window, and the prince climbed up and up and into the tower.

But instead of Rapunzel, he came face to face with the ugly old witch.

"You!" screamed the witch. "You dare to visit Rapunzel? You will never see her again!"

And she pushed the prince back out of the window. He fell down and down, right into the thorn bushes below. The sharp spikes scratched the prince's eyes and blinded him. Weeping, he stumbled away.

After months of wandering, blind and lost, the prince heard beautiful, sad singing floating through the woods. He recognized Rapunzel's voice immediately and called out to her.

Rapunzel ran to the prince and held him in her arms.

"At last, I have found you!" she said, and cried with happiness. As her tears fell onto his hurt eyes, the wounds healed and the prince could see again.

"My love!" he said, and kissed Rapunzel.

Rapunzel had never been so happy. She and the prince were soon married, and Rapunzel's parents came to the wedding. Rapunzel and the prince lived happily ever after in a grand castle, far away from the old witch and her empty tower.

The End

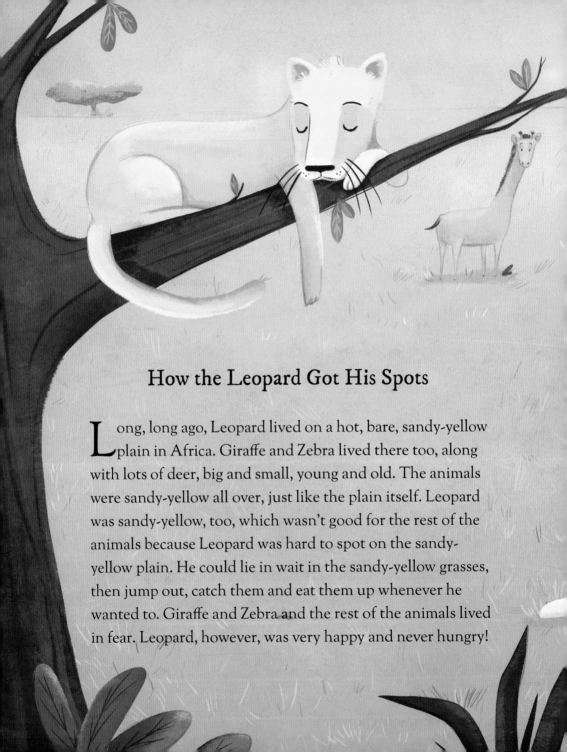

How the Leopard Got His Spots

Long, long ago, Leopard lived on a hot, bare, sandy-yellow plain in Africa. Giraffe and Zebra lived there too, along with lots of deer, big and small, young and old. The animals were sandy-yellow all over, just like the plain itself. Leopard was sandy-yellow, too, which wasn't good for the rest of the animals because Leopard was hard to spot on the sandy-yellow plain. He could lie in wait in the sandy-yellow grasses, then jump out, catch them and eat them up whenever he wanted to. Giraffe and Zebra and the rest of the animals lived in fear. Leopard, however, was very happy and never hungry!

After a while, Giraffe and Zebra and the others had had enough. They decided to move away from the sandy plain to find a better place to live. They walked and walked until they came to a huge forest where the sun shone through the trees making stripy, speckly, patchy shadows, and sections of spotty, stripy sunshine. The animals hid themselves there, and while they hid, partly in the sun, partly in the shadows, their skins changed color. Giraffe's skin became covered with big, brown, blotchy spots from the blotchy shadow he stood in, and Zebra's skin became covered with stripes from the stripy shadow he lay in. The other animals' skin became darker, too, with wavy lines and patterns from the shadows around them.

Back on the sandy plain, Leopard was puzzled. All the animals had disappeared, and he was starting to get hungry.

"Where have they all gone?" he asked Baboon.

"To the forest," said Baboon carelessly. "And they've changed. You need to change too."

Leopard started to ask Baboon what she meant by "change," but Baby Baboon needed feeding, so she was too busy to explain.

Leopard set out for the forest. He walked and walked, and at last he found it, but all he could see was tree trunks. They were speckled, spotted, dotted, and splashed with shadows. He couldn't see Giraffe or Zebra or any of the others, but he could smell them so he knew they were there.

Leopard lay down to wait. After a long, long time, something moved in the shadows and a small deer trotted toward him. But sandy-yellow Leopard wasn't hidden in the leafy, green forest, so the deer saw him at once and skipped away. All Leopard could catch was its tail.

"I'm too small to fill your belly," cried the deer. "Please, let me go."

The deer was right about that. It was tiny and thin and not really worth bothering about, but Leopard kept hold of its tail anyway.

"What's happened to all the animals?" asked Leopard.

"We've all changed," the deer replied. "Now our skins are speckly, spotty, dotty, and splashy, just like the shadows in the forest. You only caught me because I'm young. I should have been more careful."

Leopard let the little deer go and sat down to think. "So that's why I can't see Giraffe and Zebra and the rest of them in the forest," he thought. "They've changed their skins to match the shadowy trees. If I'm going to catch them, do I need to change, too? And how in the world can I do that?"

As he sat there thinking, more deer walked through the trees. When they moved, Leopard could see them clearly. When they stopped moving, they were hidden by the shadows. Leopard was easy to spot with his sandy-yellow skin, so the deer didn't come too close.

Leopard sat in the shadows a long, long time and licked his paws thoughtfully. Soon he began to notice something odd. His paws weren't sandy-yellow any more. They had small, dark spots on them. And there were spots on his tail, too.

Leopard looked around and realized that the spots on his skin matched the small, dark patches of shadow he was lying in. "Ah-ha!" he thought. "The shadows have made these spots, just in the time that I've been lying here. That's how I can change my skin, just like Giraffe and Zebra and the rest of them!"

By this time, Leopard had grown tired from all the thinking and waiting, so he lay down and fell into a deep sleep. When he awoke a long, long time later, his skin was completely covered with small, dark spots, made by the shadows of the forest.

"Well, how wonderful!" he said, looking at his new skin. "Now my skin is no longer sandy-yellow-brownish, I can hide in the leafy, green forest so that Giraffe and Zebra and the rest of them can't see me. Then, when they come close, I can leap out to catch them and eat them up!"

With that, the spotty Leopard set off into the speckly, blotchy, stripy shade of the deep forest, where he lived happily ever after, eating and sleeping and not being spotted. And the other animals learned to hide from him as best as they could, too!

The End

The Nightingale

The Emperor of China once lived in a palace so magnificent that travelers would come from all over the world just to admire it. They returned home and wrote books about the delicate porcelain palace and its beautiful garden where little silver bells were tied to the prettiest flowers and tinkled as you passed by. But most of all they wrote about the Nightingale, with his exquisite voice that brought joy to all who heard him sing.

"How can there be such a bird in my empire, in my own garden? Why has no one told me?" the Emperor exclaimed when he read their accounts. And he demanded that the Nightingale should be brought to the palace to sing for him.

The palace officials searched high and low for the Nightingale, but without success. At last they found a poor little kitchen girl who told them, "I know him well. Every evening I hear the Nightingale sing. It brings tears to my eyes." And she took them into the forest where the tiny bird willingly burst into song.

The Lord-in-Waiting was mightily impressed and invited the Nightingale to the palace. "My song is best heard in the woods," the little bird told him humbly. But when he heard it was the Emperor's wish for him to sing at the palace, the Nightingale went willingly.

There was huge excitement in the palace. The flowers with tinkling bells were brought inside the grand hall, and in the middle of the throne room where the Emperor sat, a special golden cage was arranged for the Nightingale.

When his moment came, the little bird sang so sweetly that he melted the Emperor's heart. The Emperor offered to reward him with a golden slipper, but the little bird declined.

"I have seen tears in the Emperor's eyes," he said, "I have my reward."

So he was invited to stay at court and was given his own cage. Twelve footmen took him out to fly twice a day and once at night. Each one held a ribbon tied to the Nightingale's leg. The little bird was soon the talk of the land.

One day the Emperor received an artificial nightingale encrusted with diamonds, rubies, and sapphires. When it was wound up, it sang one of the Nightingale's songs, over and over again. The courtiers soon began to prefer this bird as it sang as well as the Nightingale but looked prettier with all its sparkling jewels. So the real Nightingale flew back to his home in the forest.

The artificial bird had its own cushion beside the Emperor's bed and was given the title "Grand Imperial Singer-of-the-Emperor-to-sleep." After a year, every person in China knew the song of the artificial bird, and wherever you went, you could hear children singing, **"Zizizi! Kluk, kluk, kluk."**

But then one night, something inside the bird broke. The watchmaker warned that the bird could only sing once a year from now on, otherwise the music would stop.

Five years passed, and a real sorrow engulfed the whole country. China's much-loved Emperor now fell ill, and the country prepared for a new leader.

"Sing!" the sick Emperor called weakly to the artificial bird. "Sing, my little bird! I have given you gold and precious presents. Sing, I pray you, sing!"

But the bird stood silent.

Suddenly, through the window came a burst of song. It was the real Nightingale. And as he sang, the blood flowed quicker and quicker through the Emperor's feeble body.

"Thank you, thank you!" the Emperor cried. "Little bird from Heaven, you have sung away the sadness. How can I ever repay you?"

"You have already rewarded me," said the Nightingale. "I brought tears to your eyes when first I sang for you. Sleep now, and grow fresh and strong while I sing."

"You must stay with me always," said the Emperor. "I shall break the artificial bird into a thousand pieces."

"No," said the Nightingale. "It did its best. Keep it near you. I cannot live in a palace, so let me come as I will. Then I shall sit by your window and sing things that will make you happy. A little singing bird flies far and wide, to the fisherman's hut, to the farmer's home, and to many other places a long way off. I will come and sing to you, if you will promise me one thing."

"All that I have is yours," cried the Emperor.

"You must not let anyone know that you have a little bird who tells you everything." And away he flew.

Early the next day, when the servants came expecting to find their Emperor very sick, they were astonished to hear him speak.

"Good morning," he said, standing proudly in all his fine robes.

The End

Sleeping Beauty

Once upon a time, there lived a king and queen. When the queen gave birth to a beautiful baby girl, the king and queen were filled with joy and decided to hold a christening feast to celebrate. They invited their friends, and all the kings, queens, princes, and princesses from other kingdoms all over the land.

Five good fairies lived in the kingdom, and the king wanted them to be godmothers to his daughter. One of these fairies was very old, and no one had seen her in years or even knew where she was. So when the king sent out the invitations to his daughter's christening, he invited only the four young fairies.

The day of the christening arrived. It was a joyous occasion, and the palace was full of laughter and dancing.

After the delicious feast, the four good fairies gave the princess their magical gifts.

Bending over the crib, the first fairy waved her wand and said, "You shall be kind and considerate."

The second fairy said, "You shall be beautiful and loving."

The third fairy said, "You shall be clever and thoughtful."

The baby girl was promised everything in the world that you could wish for. But just as the third fairy finished giving her gift, there was a loud bang, and the palace doors flew open.

It was the old fairy. She was furious because she hadn't been invited to the feast. She rushed over to the sleeping baby and waved her wand, casting a curse upon the child.

"One day the king's daughter shall prick her finger on a spindle and fall down dead!" she screeched.

And then she left.

The guests fell silent at these terrible words, and the queen burst into tears.

The fourth fairy had not yet given her gift. "Dear Queen, please do not weep. I cannot undo the curse, but I can soften it," she said.

She walked to the crib and waved her wand.

"The princess will prick her finger on a spindle, but she will not die. Instead, the princess and everyone within the palace and its grounds will fall into a deep sleep that will last for one hundred years."

The king thanked the fairy for her kindness and then, to protect his daughter, ordered that every spindle in the kingdom be burned.

The years passed, and the princess grew into a beautiful and kind young woman, just as the fairies had promised.

One day, to amuse herself, the princess decided to explore the rooms in the palace that she had never been in before.

After a while, she came to a little door at the top of a tall tower. Inside, there was an old woman working at her spinning wheel. The princess didn't know that the woman was really the old fairy in disguise.

"What are you doing?" the princess asked curiously.

"I'm spinning thread, dear child," replied the woman.

"Can I try?" said the princess.

No sooner had she touched the spindle than she pricked her finger and fell into a deep, deep sleep.

A strange quietness came over the palace, from the gardens to the tallest tower, and the king and queen began to yawn.

Before long, every living thing within the castle walls had fallen into a deep, deep sleep.

As time passed, a hedge of thorns sprang up around the palace. It grew higher and thicker every year, until only the tallest towers could be seen above it.

The story of the beautiful princess that lay sleeping within its walls spread throughout the land. She became known as Sleeping Beauty.

Many princes tried to break through the thorns to rescue Sleeping Beauty, but none were successful. The thorn hedge was too thick.

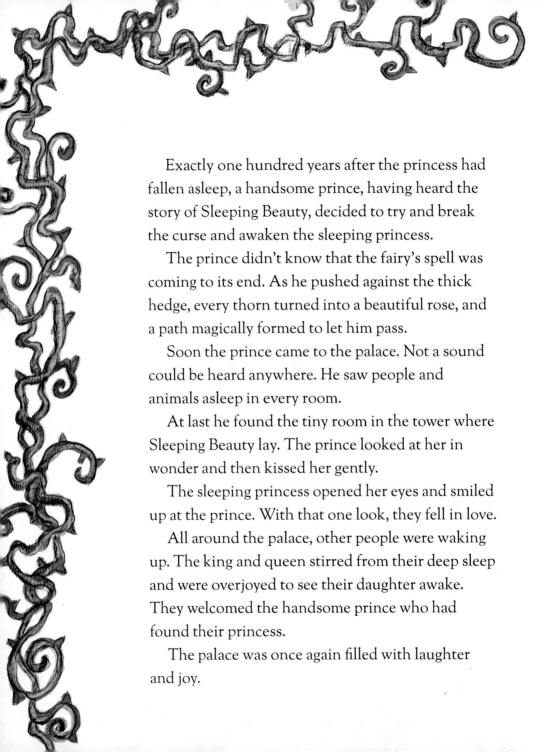

Exactly one hundred years after the princess had fallen asleep, a handsome prince, having heard the story of Sleeping Beauty, decided to try and break the curse and awaken the sleeping princess.

The prince didn't know that the fairy's spell was coming to its end. As he pushed against the thick hedge, every thorn turned into a beautiful rose, and a path magically formed to let him pass.

Soon the prince came to the palace. Not a sound could be heard anywhere. He saw people and animals asleep in every room.

At last he found the tiny room in the tower where Sleeping Beauty lay. The prince looked at her in wonder and then kissed her gently.

The sleeping princess opened her eyes and smiled up at the prince. With that one look, they fell in love.

All around the palace, other people were waking up. The king and queen stirred from their deep sleep and were overjoyed to see their daughter awake. They welcomed the handsome prince who had found their princess.

The palace was once again filled with laughter and joy.

The king called for a huge wedding feast to be prepared, and he invited everyone in the entire kingdom.

Sleeping Beauty married her handsome prince, and they lived happily ever after.

The End

Peter and the Wolf

Peter lived with his grandfather in a little cottage in the valley. Grandfather taught him to be kind to the animals, and Peter soon became friends with many woodland creatures.

Grandfather also taught Peter about the dangers of living in the woods and how he must always be on the alert for wolves. Which is why Grandfather insisted that the cottage gate was kept closed.

Early one morning, Peter woke before Grandfather, and as the sun was starting to rise above the mountains, he set off to play. Peter was so eager that he forgot to close the gate. He ran into the big green meadow. Seeing the gate wide open, the duck waddled through the yard and followed Peter.

Peter headed for his favorite tree, where his friend, a little bird, was perched.

"Morning Peter," the bird chirped happily.

Peter climbed onto the lower branch and started chatting. Everywhere was so quiet, there wasn't even a ripple on the pond in the meadow.

Then suddenly they heard an excited **"Quack!"**

"Oh, no, I forgot to close the gate!" cried Peter. "Why did you follow me?" he asked the excited duck. "Grandfather is going to be so cross."

"Quack! Quack!" replied Duck, heading straight for the pond.

Now Duck and the little bird always found something to argue about. As Duck waddled along, the little bird joined him.

"What kind of a bird are you if you can't fly?" he chirped.

"And what kind of a bird are you if you can't swim?" replied the duck before diving into the pond with a big splash. And as the duck swam and the bird hopped along the side of the pond, they continued to argue.

Suddenly Peter noticed a cat ready to pounce on the bird.

"Look out!" cried Peter. And in a flash, the little bird was back in the tree again.

The cat stared in surprise as the duck flapped her wings wildly. Then the cat turned his attention to the bird once more and began to circle the tree. He wondered if he could climb up quickly enough to catch the little creature before it flew away again.

"It certainly isn't quiet any more," smiled Peter as he watched in amusement. But then an angry voice made him jump.

"Peter! Peter, how could you leave the gate open?" cried Grandfather, running across the meadow. "What if a wolf had come?"

"Boys like me are not afraid of wolves," replied Peter. But Grandfather did not want to hear this.

He led Peter across the meadow, and back to the cottage. As Peter waited behind the gate, he realized that Grandfather did know best. For at that moment, a big gray wolf appeared.

Seeing the little duck swimming on the pond, the wolf bared his teeth and licked his lips. The duck jumped out of the pond in fright at the sight of the wolf. And in no time, the wolf was chasing the little duck across the field. No matter how hard she ran, she couldn't escape from the wolf. Nearer and nearer came the wolf until **SNAP!** The duck disappeared.

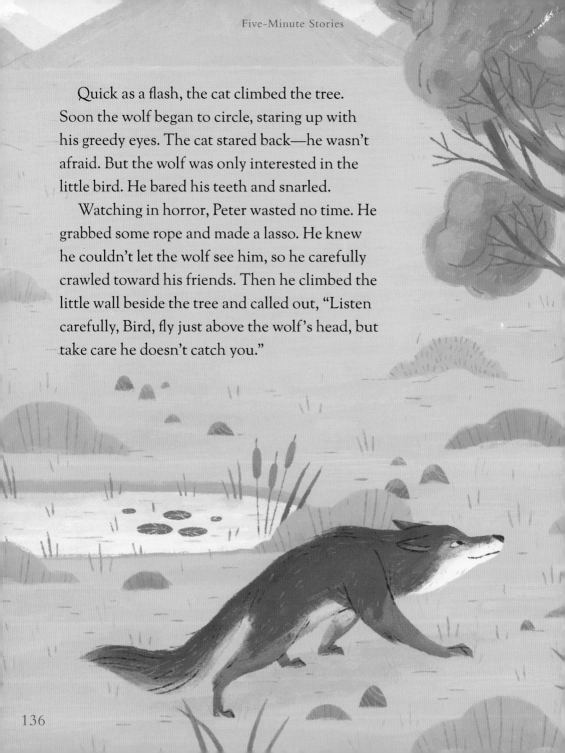

Quick as a flash, the cat climbed the tree. Soon the wolf began to circle, staring up with his greedy eyes. The cat stared back—he wasn't afraid. But the wolf was only interested in the little bird. He bared his teeth and snarled.

Watching in horror, Peter wasted no time. He grabbed some rope and made a lasso. He knew he couldn't let the wolf see him, so he carefully crawled toward his friends. Then he climbed the little wall beside the tree and called out, "Listen carefully, Bird, fly just above the wolf's head, but take care he doesn't catch you."

The little bird did as he was told. As the wolf snapped, the bird swooped up and down, just out of reach. While the clever bird distracted the wolf, Peter leapt on to the tree.

He tied the end of the rope to a branch and dropped the lasso over the wolf's tail. The more the wolf jumped, the more the rope tightened around his tail. And the more angry he became.

Just then some hunters appeared, following the trail of the wolf.

"We've caught the wolf!" cried Peter. "Help us to take him to the zoo."

The hunters were happy to help. At the head of the group was Peter, followed by the hunters leading the wolf. Grandfather trailed along at the back, still cross with Peter for disobeying him.

"If Peter hadn't caught the wolf, what then?" grumbled Grandfather. He was not happy that Peter took such a risk.

"But Peter and I were too clever for the wolf," the little bird told Grandfather.

Now if you listened very carefully as the group passed by, you would just hear a faint **"Quack!"** The wolf was in such a hurry when he ate the duck that he swallowed the bird whole, and the brave creature was still alive.

The End

Aladdin

Once upon a time, a boy named Aladdin lived with his mother. They were so poor that every day it was a struggle to find enough money for food.

One day a man came to their shack saying he was Aladdin's long-lost uncle. When he said he would help Aladdin make his fortune, Aladdin and his mother were delighted.

Aladdin traveled with him into the desert until they came to a rock. The man pushed it aside, revealing a hidden cave.

"You must climb down into this cave and fetch a lamp that you will find there," he said. "Bring it to me. Don't touch anything except the lamp. Wear this magic ring to protect you."

Aladdin was afraid, but he dared not argue with his uncle. He put on the magic ring and climbed into the cave. As soon as he was through the entrance his eyes grew wide with wonder. All around, piles of gold and jewels stretched from floor to ceiling. Gemstones glittered in the dim light. Just one ruby would make Aladdin and his mother rich. But he did as he had promised and touched nothing. At last he found a dull, brass lamp.

"Surely this can't be it?" Aladdin thought, but he took it back to his uncle. When he got to the opening, he found he couldn't climb out of the cave holding the lamp.

"Pass it to me," his uncle said, "then I will help you out."

"Help me out first, uncle," Aladdin replied, "and then I will give you the lamp."

"No!" the man shouted. "First give me the lamp!"

When Aladdin refused, the man became angry. He rolled the stone over the opening to the cave, trapping Aladdin in the dark.

"Uncle!" Aladdin shouted. "Let me out!"

"Hah!" the man shouted back. "I'm not your uncle, fool! I'm a sorcerer! You can stay there and die, if you won't give me the lamp!"

Aladdin wrung his hands in despair. As he did so, he rubbed the magic ring the sorcerer had given him for protection. Suddenly, a genie sprang out.

"I am the genie of the ring. What do you require, oh master?" The genie bowed. Aladdin was astonished, but he thought quickly.

"Please take me home to my mother," he said. And immediately he was outside his mother's house. He told her everything that had happened, and she hugged him with relief.

"Oh, but Aladdin," she cried, "we are still poor!"

The next day, Aladdin looked at the lamp he had fetched from the cave. "It doesn't look like much," he thought, and he started to polish it, hoping he could sell it to get money for food. As soon as he rubbed the lamp, another genie appeared.

"I am the genie of the lamp. What do you require, oh lord?" the genie asked. This time, Aladdin knew what to do. He asked the genie to bring food and money so that he and his mother could live in comfort.

Life went on happily, until one day Aladdin saw the beautiful daughter of the emperor. He fell in love and felt that he couldn't live without her. But how could he marry a princess?

Aladdin thought and thought, and finally he had an idea. He asked the genie for beautiful gifts to give to the princess.

When the princess spoke to Aladdin to thank him for the gifts, she fell in love with him. They were married, and Aladdin asked the genie to build them a beautiful palace.

Hearing that a wealthy stranger had married the princess, the sorcerer guessed that Aladdin must have escaped from the cave with the lamp.

One day, when Aladdin was out, the sorcerer disguised himself as a poor tradesman. He stood outside the palace calling out, "New lamps for old! New lamps for old!"

Aladdin's wife remembered the ugly brass lamp that Aladdin kept and took it to the man. The sorcerer snatched it from her, rubbed the lamp and commanded the genie to carry the palace and the princess far away to his own home in another country.

"Where is my beautiful wife?" cried Aladdin when he returned home, wringing his hands in despair. As he did so, he rubbed the ring and the first genie appeared.

"What do you require, master?" the genie of the ring asked.

"Please bring back my wife and palace!" Aladdin pleaded. But the genie of the ring was less powerful than the genie of the lamp.

"Then take me to her so that I can win her back!" Aladdin said.

At once, he found himself in a strange city, but outside his own palace. Through a window he saw his wife crying, and the sorcerer sleeping. Furious, Aladdin climbed in through a window and crept to the bedroom. He slipped the magic lamp from beneath the sorcerer's pillow and rubbed it.

"What do you require, master?" asked the genie.

"Take us straight back home," Aladdin said. "And shut this sorcerer in the cave for a thousand years—that will teach him a lesson!"

In a moment, the palace was back where it belonged. With the sorcerer gone, Aladdin and the princess were safe again. They lived long and happy lives together and never needed to call on the genie again.

The End

The Flying Trunk

Once there was a merchant so rich he could have paved a street with silver, but instead he chose to leave all his money to his idle son. After enjoying the high life, the son soon found that all his father's money had vanished. His friends disappeared too, but one sent him an old trunk with a note saying, **"Pack up and be off!"**

The merchant's son was amazed to discover that the trunk could fly. So he climbed in, closed the lid, and flew high into the sky, leaving his troubles behind.

At last the trunk descended and he found himself in a foreign land. Hiding the trunk in a forest, he walked into the town.

"Who lives in that palace?" he asked a stranger, pointing up to the hill.

"The King's daughter," came the reply. "It has been prophesied that a man will make her unhappy, so no one is allowed to visit, except the King and Queen."

Hearing this, the merchant's son had an idea. That evening he flew up to the palace roof and into the princess' room. He was immediately struck by her beauty.

"Do not be afraid," he told her gently. "I am a prophet descended from the sky."

The lonely princess was excited to have company. She was entranced by the stranger's tales of mermaids in dark-blue seas and princesses on magical snow-clad mountains. She believed this prophet had been sent just for her and readily agreed to his proposal.

"But first you must come here on Saturday," she told him. "The King and Queen will be pleased to hear I am to marry a prophet." And then she gave him some advice. "They are exceedingly fond of stories. My mother likes them to be moral and my father likes them to be merry."

"I shall bring a tale as my bridal present," he replied confidently. And before he flew away, the princess gave him a gift of a saber studded with gold.

"I shall exchange this for more fine clothes," he thought as he waved his princess farewell.

Saturday soon arrived, and the
princess proudly introduced her
prophet to the King and Queen, who
invited him to tell them a story.

"There was once a bundle of matches,"
he began. "They lay on a mantelpiece
between a tinderbox and an old iron
saucepan. They often talked about
their youth."

The King and Queen smiled
with approval.

The prophet continued his tale.

"The matches were proud they were once branches on a fir tree that towered above all other trees. They boasted how the trunk of the tree became a mainmast of a magnificent ship that sailed around the world. And they told how the birds would relate stories of far off lands they had visited. Which is why the matches felt they were above living in a kitchen."

The Queen, who loved a moral tale, applauded when she heard this.

"But where is the merriment?" asked the King.

"Soon," replied the prophet, continuing.

"'My story is very simple,' said the iron saucepan. 'I have been rubbed and scrubbed and boiled over and over again. We lead a quiet life here, but the newcomer, the turf-basket, tells such terrible tales that the old glass jar fell down in shock and shattered into a thousand pieces.'"

The King laughed out loud.

"When the jug told her story," continued the prophet, "the plates all clattered applause and the fire-tongs began to dance. The kettle was asked to sing, but she had a cold so could only sing when she was boiling. Before anyone else could tell their tale, the maid came in to light the fire and struck one of the matches. How it blazed up.

"'Now,' thought the other matches, 'everyone can see we are of the highest rank as we bring a dazzling light.'"

The King and Queen applauded loudly.

"You shall marry our daughter on Monday," the King declared.

The night before the wedding the whole city was illuminated, and cakes and buns and sugarplums were thrown to the people in the street.

"I should play my part," thought the merchant's son, so he bought some fireworks and let them off one by one as he flew into the air in his trunk.

The crowd jumped and roared with delight as rockets and fountains of light filled the sky in honor of their princess marrying a prophet.

Later, the merchant's son set off into the city.

"I saw the prophet," one of the crowd told him, "he had eyes like sparkling stars and a beard like foaming water."

Happy with his evening's work and excited about his marriage the next day, the merchant's son returned to the forest. But disaster faced him. One spark from a firework had ignited the trunk and it now lay in ashes. The merchant's son could never fly again and could never visit his bride.

Every day the princess sat on the palace roof waiting for her prophet. And he traveled the world telling stories, but they were never as happy as the ones he told at the princess' palace.

The End

153

Tom Thumb

There was once a poor farmer and his wife who loved each other dearly. But there was one thing missing from their lives.

"How happy I should be if I had but one child," the wife told her husband. "Even if it were no bigger than my thumb, I should love it with all my heart."

So when the wife heard about the great magician Merlin at the court of King Arthur, she persuaded her husband to pay him a visit. Merlin agreed to help, and months later the wife had a little boy, no bigger than his father's thumb. They named him Tom Thumb.

Tom was a clever boy and always eager to help his parents. One day as his father struggled with the cart, Tom had an idea.

"Let me get into the horse's ear and tell him which way to go," he suggested excitedly. So Tom gave the instructions, and the horse obeyed.

Watching from the road were two strangers.

"How odd," said one, "that cart is moving and I can hear a voice, but I can't see anyone driving."

The men followed the cart and soon heard Tom calling, "See father, I did it." And to their astonishment, the old man lifted the tiny boy out of the horse's ear.

The men approached asking if they could buy Tom as they could see he would make them a fortune. At first the farmer refused, but Tom wanted the best for his parents.

"Take the money, father," he said. "I promise I will soon come back to you."

So, reluctantly, the old farmer handed Tom to the strangers for a tidy sum of money.

As they set off, Tom sat perched on one of the men's hats, figuring out his plan. When they finally stopped, he wasted no time, jumping down and running straight into the first mouse-hole he saw. The two men tried in vain to reach him, but the hole was too small for their hands. Furious, they were forced to give up.

Tom then crept out and found an empty snail shell, where he fell asleep. He was woken by whispering.

"There's the parson's house. Let's steal his gold and silver," said one voice.

"But how?" asked another.

Sitting up, Tom could just make out two men in dark clothes.

"Take me with you and I'll show you how to get into the parson's house," called Tom.

The men were startled to see such a small creature.

"I can get into the house without being seen," explained Tom, "and pass out all the valuables."

So Tom went along with the thieves and found himself standing in the hall of the parson's house.

"Do you want this candelabra?" shouted Tom through the window.

"Keep your voice down," came the whispered reply. But Tom continued to make a noise, hoping to wake someone.

It was the cook who woke first. Hearing a clatter and the sound of voices, she sprang out of bed. She failed to notice Tom in the hall, but when the thieves saw her at the door, they raced away.

Pleased with his work, Tom crept outside and spent the night in the hayloft.

Early the next morning, the maid picked up a bundle of hay to feed to the cows. Little did she know that she had picked up the tiny boy, too. And soon he was swallowed by a hungry cow.

Tom's cries were drowned out by the loud **"Moo!"** from the cow as she continued to chew the hay happily.

Only later, as the maid finished milking, did she hear Tom calling, "I'm inside the cow!"

The startled maid ran to fetch the parson. It wasn't an easy task, but finally Tom was freed. And yet, his adventures did not stop there.

For just as Tom was crossing a field, he was spotted by a wolf lurking in the trees.

Quick as a flash, the hungry wolf sprang out of the woods and pounced on poor Tom, swallowing him whole. But the clever little boy did not give up. He had a plan.

"My good friend, how would you like a feast?" he called out.

The wolf could not resist. "A feast you say?" he replied eagerly.

"With, ham, beef, cold chicken, cake, and every delight you could wish for," replied Tom, directing the wolf to his parents' house.

Arriving there, the wolf headed straight for the pantry. He ate and ate and ate and soon needed to lie down. Inside the wolf's tummy, Tom began to sing very loudly.

"Keep quiet," snapped the wolf, but Tom continued. And his trick worked.

160

The farmer's wife woke and called her husband. As they peeped into the kitchen, they were horrified to see a wolf sleeping by the pantry door. As the farmer grabbed his axe, he was amazed to hear Tom calling out, "Father, Father! I am inside the wolf."

So the farmer struck the wolf on the head. Minutes later, to the delight of his parents, Tom Thumb was sitting on the kitchen table telling them all about his adventures.

"I have been down a mouse-hole, slept in a snail shell, been eaten first by a cow and then a wolf," he laughed.

"And now you are home," cried his mother happily. And they all agreed, there was no place better than home.

The End

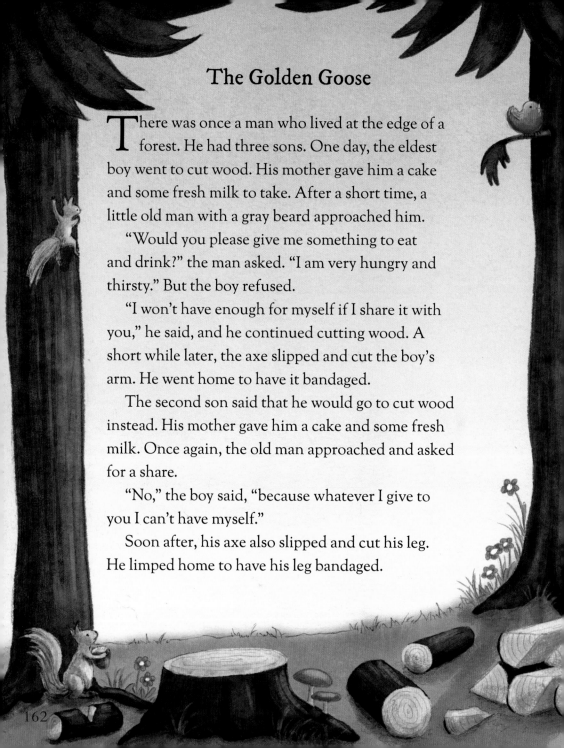

The Golden Goose

There was once a man who lived at the edge of a forest. He had three sons. One day, the eldest boy went to cut wood. His mother gave him a cake and some fresh milk to take. After a short time, a little old man with a gray beard approached him.

"Would you please give me something to eat and drink?" the man asked. "I am very hungry and thirsty." But the boy refused.

"I won't have enough for myself if I share it with you," he said, and he continued cutting wood. A short while later, the axe slipped and cut the boy's arm. He went home to have it bandaged.

The second son said that he would go to cut wood instead. His mother gave him a cake and some fresh milk. Once again, the old man approached and asked for a share.

"No," the boy said, "because whatever I give to you I can't have myself."

Soon after, his axe also slipped and cut his leg. He limped home to have his leg bandaged.

The youngest boy, Billy, then said that he would go to cut wood. His father refused.

"You are a silly boy. Your brothers have hurt themselves, so you certainly will too," he said.

But Billy insisted. At last, his mother gave him a dry biscuit and a bottle of plain water, and he set off into the forest. No sooner had he started work than the old man appeared and asked for a drink and a bite to eat.

"It's plain food," Billy said, "but if you're happy with dry biscuit and water, I'll gladly share with you."

They shared the biscuit and water, then the little old man said, "You have been good to me, and you will have your reward. Cut down that tree over there and see what you find inside it."

Billy did as the man said. Hidden inside the tree trunk he found a goose with shining feathers of pure gold! Billy wondered how there could be such a strange bird. He looked around for the old man, but he had vanished, so Billy picked up the goose and set off for home.

Before long, Billy was totally lost. It was growing dark, so when he came to an inn he decided to stay the night.

The innkeeper had three daughters. They were very curious about the golden goose. When Billy went for supper, the eldest girl thought she would steal a single feather. As soon as she put her hand on the goose, she stuck fast to it! No matter how she struggled, she couldn't get free.

The middle girl, also wanting a feather, tried to push her sister out of the way, but found that she became stuck fast to her sister's arm.

When the youngest girl approached, her sisters warned her not to touch them. But she thought they were trying to keep the golden feathers all for themselves. She took hold of the middle sister's arm, and immediately she stuck like glue.

The next morning, Billy set off down the street with the golden goose, dragging the girls behind him. As they passed a church, the parson called out, "What are you girls doing, running after that young man? Let go at once!"

He tried to pull the youngest girl away, but he was then as stuck as they were. The parson called to his wife to free him, but that just ended with the wife sticking to the parson.

Two farmers ran from their fields to help the strange group, and soon they were stuck fast, too.

By now there were seven people in a line following behind the boy with his golden goose. It was the strangest procession you could imagine!

It happened that they passed near the king's palace. He had a daughter, but she was always miserable. No one could make the princess smile, let alone laugh. The king was so desperate to cheer her up that he had promised her hand in marriage to anyone who could make her happy. Many young men had tried to amuse her, telling jokes, doing tricks, fooling around, and making faces, but nothing worked—she was as sad as ever.

When the princess looked out of her window that day and saw Billy walking along the street carrying a golden goose, she started to smile.

Then she saw the three sisters, the parson, the parson's wife, and the two farmers staggering along behind. Her smile turned to a laugh, and her laugh became louder and louder. She laughed so hard that tears ran down her cheeks.

"My dear, what has made you laugh?" the king cried, delighted. The princess was laughing so much she couldn't speak. She could only point at Billy and the long line of people stuck to the goose.

The king sent a footman to bring Billy to the palace.

"The princess is laughing!" the king exclaimed. "You made her laugh! That means you may marry her!"

"I? Marry the princess?" Billy said.

"Why, yes," the king answered.
"I am so glad that at last someone
has helped my poor, sad daughter.
All I want is for her to be happy—if you
can make her smile and laugh, you are
the best husband she could have."

Suddenly the golden goose jumped
from Billy's arms, and all the people
toppled backward, unstuck.

Billy and the princess soon married,
and they lived long, happy lives
full of smiles and laughter.

The End

Jack and the Beanstalk

Once upon a time, there was a young boy named Jack, who lived with his mother in a cottage. They were so poor that, bit by bit, they had to sell everything they owned just to buy their food. Then one day, Jack's mother said to him,

"We will have to sell Bluebell, our old cow. Take her to the market, Jack, and remember to sell her for a good price."

So Jack took Bluebell off to market. He had just reached the edge of the town when an old man appeared at the side of the road.

"Are you going to sell that fine cow?" said the man.

"Yes," said Jack.

"Well, I'll buy her from you, and I'll give you these magic beans," said the man, holding out a handful of dry beans. "They don't look like much, but if you plant them, you and your mother will be rich beyond your wildest dreams."

Jack liked the sound of being rich. And he didn't even stop to wonder how this stranger knew about his mother!

"It's a deal!" he said. He gave Bluebell to the man and took the beans.

When Jack showed his mother the beans, she was so angry that her face turned as red as a beetroot!

"You stupid boy! Go to your room!" she cried, and threw the beans out of the window.

Jack sat on his bed, feeling miserable. "Stupid beans," he muttered. "Stupid me!" Then he fell asleep.

When Jack woke up the next morning, it was strangely dark in his room, and all he could see through the window were the leaves of a huge plant. A plant so tall that he couldn't see the top of it.

"It must be a magic beanstalk!" cried Jack. "What's at the top?"

So Jack started to climb. Up he went, from branch to branch and from leaf to leaf. At the top was a giant house. Jack's tummy was rumbling with hunger, so he knocked on the great big door. A giant woman answered.

"Please, madam, may I have some breakfast?" Jack asked politely.

"You'll become breakfast if my husband finds you!" said the giant's wife. But Jack begged and pleaded, and at last she let him in and gave him some bread and milk.

The giant's wife had just shown Jack where to hide when the giant came home in a bad mood.

"Fee, fi, fo, fum, I smell the blood of an Englishman!" roared the giant.

"Silly man," said his wife. "You smell the sausages I have cooked you for breakfast."

The giant ate a giant-sized breakfast, then settled down to count the huge gold coins in his treasure chest. There were lots of coins. "One hundred and one ... one hundred and two ..." he counted, but his head started to nod and before long he was fast asleep.

Quick as a flash, Jack grabbed two of the huge gold coins and ran out through the front door. He raced to the beanstalk and climbed down it as fast as his legs would carry him.

His mother was so happy to see the gold that she hugged Jack for ten whole minutes!

"Clever boy, Jack!" she laughed. "We'll never be poor again!"

Before long, however, Jack and his mother had spent all the money, so the boy decided to climb the beanstalk again. Just as before, Jack knocked on the door and asked the giant's wife for some food. He begged and he pleaded, and at last she let him in. She gave him some bread and milk and hid him in the cupboard just as the giant arrived home.

When the giant had eaten a giant-sized lunch, his wife brought him his pet hen. **"Lay!"** he bellowed, and the hen laid a solid gold egg. It laid ten eggs before the giant started to snore. Jack could hardly believe his luck! Quick as a flash, he picked up the hen and ran.

When his mother saw the hen lay a golden egg, she hugged Jack for twenty whole minutes!

Although Jack and his mother were now rich beyond their wildest dreams, the boy couldn't help himself—he decided to climb the beanstalk one more time.

This time, Jack knew that the giant's wife would not be happy to see him, so he sneaked in when she wasn't looking and quickly hid in the cupboard. The giant came home as usual and ate a giant-sized dinner, then his wife brought him his magic harp.

"Play!" he roared, and the harp began to play. It was such sweet music that the giant fell asleep in record time!

Jack grabbed the harp and started to run, but the harp cried out, "Master! Help!"

The giant woke up at once and chased after Jack. The boy slithered down the beanstalk faster than he'd ever done before, but the giant was catching up!

"Mother, fetch me the axe!" Jack yelled as he reached the ground. Then he chopped at the beanstalk with all his might.

Creak! Groan! The giant quickly climbed back up to the top just before the beanstalk crashed to the ground. When his mother heard the harp play, she hugged Jack for a whole hour! And, as you can imagine, the two of them lived happily ever after.

The End

The Steadfast Tin Soldier

There was once a little boy who was given a whole army of toy soldiers for his birthday. He was bursting with excitement as he lined them all up in their matching red and blue uniforms. Each one had a musket over his shoulder. The last soldier to be made only had one leg as the toymaker had run out of tin. But this one-legged soldier stood just as proud as all the others.

The one-legged soldier admired a pretty ballerina standing in the boy's castle. She was cut out of paper and wore a delicate dress and a sparkling sash. But what struck him most was that she was standing on just one leg.

"She's just like me," he thought, not realizing that she actually had two legs.

When the boy marched his soldiers back into their box, the one-legged soldier hid, hoping to talk to the ballerina.

Later, when the boy went to bed, all the toys magically came to life. The jack-in-the-box sprang out of his box, the steam train chugged around, and the ballerina started dancing.

The soldier was entranced.

"She's the most beautiful girl I've ever seen," he said to himself as she twirled gracefully around and around. Just for a moment, he thought she might have glanced his way, too.

"She wouldn't care for you with just one leg!" the jack-in-the-box suddenly hissed, clearly feeling jealous.

Sadly, the soldier realized that the jack-in-the-box was probably right. Why would someone so beautiful and living in a castle care for him? Nevertheless, he still could not take his eyes off her.

"Don't get ideas above your rank," said the jack-in-the-box. "You have been warned!"

The very next morning when the boy came into the nursery, he found the one-legged soldier lying on the floor. He picked him up and laid him on the window ledge. A moment later, a gust of wind caught the soldier. He wobbled and wobbled, then fell out of the window.

Down, down, down, he tumbled until he lay on the pavement, holding on to his musket.

The boy rushed out to look for him, but the soldier was too proud to call for help. As rain started to pour down, the boy went back inside.

"It's true, a soldier should know his place," he thought. "The beautiful ballerina would never be interested in me."

When the rain finally stopped, two boys came out to play.

"Look, it's a soldier!" one cried.

"Let's make him a boat," cried the other.

Carefully folding some newspaper, they tucked the soldier inside and sent him sailing down the gutter.

As the little paper boat rocked from side to side, the soldier held his musket tightly.

Suddenly the boat began to spin and the brave soldier found himself in the darkness of a sewer. He could just make out a pair of glinting eyes ahead.

"How dare you come into our sewer," snapped an unfriendly rat. Soon the brave soldier was being chased by a pack of rats, but just in time, a glimmer of light appeared ahead. The boat was immediately flung into the air before it crashed into the canal and fell apart. As the little soldier sank to the bottom, he still clung to his musket.

"Will I ever see my ballerina again?" was his only thought.

And at that moment a huge fish appeared, jaws wide open. **SNAP!** The one-legged soldier was now deep inside the fish's dark, scary belly. Exhausted, he soon drifted off to sleep.

He was woken by the sound of voices, and then there was a sudden flash of light. Peering down at him was the startled kitchen maid. By chance, she had bought the fish at the market.

"Well I never!" she exclaimed. And, wiping him clean, she took him upstairs to the nursery.

Everyone made a huge fuss over the returning traveler.

"Welcome back!" boomed the General. "Tell us about your adventures."

But before he had a chance, the boy burst through the door. He picked up his one-legged soldier and then hurled him into the blazing fire.

Everyone thought the boy was being spiteful. No one realized that the jealous jack-in-the-box had noticed the ballerina gently touch her heart as the soldier returned. He was the one responsible for making the soldier suddenly fly out of the boy's hand. And he was not content to stop there. He then made the nursery door fly open, causing a gust of wind that blew the ballerina into the fire as well. The soldier tried to protect her, wrapping himself around her fragile paper body, but the heat was too great.

By the time the maid came to sweep up, the tin soldier and the ballerina were gone. All that was left behind was a little tin heart, glowing in the ashes.

The End

Cinderella

Once upon a time, there was a young girl who lived with her widowed father. Eventually her father remarried. His new wife had two daughters of her own. She was mean and spiteful to the young girl, and so were her daughters. They made the girl do all the housework, eat scraps, and sleep by the fireplace among the cinders and ashes. Because she slept in the cinders, they named her "Cinderella."

One day, a letter arrived from the palace. All the women in the land were invited to attend a grand ball—where the prince would choose a bride!

Cinderella's stepsisters were very excited. Her stepmother was sure one of her daughters would marry the prince. She made Cinderella work night and day to make them as beautiful as possible. Cinderella washed and curled their dull hair. She cut and shaped their ragged nails. She stitched their ballgowns, and she polished their dancing shoes until they shone.

Cinderella longed to go to the ball herself, but her stepsisters just laughed.

"You? Go to a ball?" the elder stepsister said. "But you don't have a pretty dress!"

"How ridiculous!" laughed the younger stepsister. "You are always covered with soot and cinders!"

Tears ran down Cinderella's face as she helped her stepsisters into their dresses and jewels. At last they left for the ball. Cinderella sat alone by the fireplace. She cried and cried.

"If only I could go to the ball," she said through her tears, "and be happy for just one night. I so wish I could go."

Cinderella had barely finished speaking when there was a sparkle of light in the dull kitchen, and there stood—a fairy!

"Don't be afraid, my dear. I am your fairy godmother," the fairy said, "and you shall go to the ball!"

Cinderella stared in amazement at the fairy. Quickly, she dried her eyes.

"Really? Can I really go to the ball?" she asked, barely daring to believe it.

"If you do as I say, all will be well," the fairy answered.

"I'm used to doing as I'm told," Cinderella sniffed.

The fairy godmother told her to bring a pumpkin, four white mice, and a black rat. Cinderella hurried to the garden to pick a pumpkin. She found four mice in the kitchen, and she caught a rat sleeping in the barn. With a wave of the fairy's wand, the pumpkin turned into a gleaming golden coach. Cinderella gasped in astonishment.

"It's beautiful!" she said. "But who will drive it?"

The fairy waved her wand again, and the four mice became four handsome white horses. She waved her wand a third time, and the rat turned into a tall coachman.

184

"How wonderful!" Cinderella cried. "But I can't go to the ball in these rags."

"And you won't go in rags!" her fairy godmother cried.

She waved her wand, and Cinderella's rags turned into a beautiful ballgown. Glittering glass slippers appeared on her feet. Cinderella looked lovely!

"Now, off you go," her fairy godmother said, "but remember, all this will vanish at midnight, so make sure you are home by then."

Cinderella climbed into the coach, and it whisked her away to the palace. She had never been happier.

Everyone was enchanted by the lovely stranger, especially the prince, who danced with her all evening. Cinderella enjoyed herself so much that she completely forgot her fairy godmother's warning. Suddenly, the palace clock began to strike midnight.

Bong, bong, bong …

Cinderella picked up her skirts and fled. The worried prince ran after her.

Bong, bong, bong …

She ran down the palace steps. She lost one of her glass slippers on the way, but she didn't dare stop.

Bong, bong, bong …

Cinderella jumped into the coach, and it drove off before the prince could stop her.

Bong, bong, bong!

On the final stroke of midnight, Cinderella found herself sitting on the road beside a pumpkin. Four white mice and a black rat scampered around her. She was dressed in rags and had only a single glass slipper left from her magical evening.

"Even if it was a dream," she said to herself, "it was a perfect dream."

At the palace, the prince looked longingly at the glass slipper he had found on the steps. He could not forget the wonderful girl he had danced with all night.

"I will find her," he said to himself, "and I will marry her!"

So he took the glass slipper and set out to visit every house in the land. At last he came to Cinderella's house. Her two stepsisters tried and tried to squeeze their huge feet into the delicate slipper, but no matter what they did, they could not get the slipper to fit. Cinderella watched as she scrubbed the floor.

"May I try, please?" she asked.

"You?" laughed the eldest. "You didn't even go to the ball!"

"Everyone may try," the prince said. Cinderella sat down. Her foot slipped easily into the glass slipper.

The prince took Cinderella in his arms.

"You're the one!" he said. "Will you marry me? Please?"

Cinderella's stepmother and stepsisters were furious.

"It can't be her!"

"She's just the servant!"

"She dresses in rags!"

But at that moment, the fairy godmother appeared and turned Cinderella's rags back into the fabulous ballgown. Cinderella took the other slipper from her pocket.

"Yes," Cinderella said. "Yes, it was me, and yes I will marry you."

Much to the disgust of her stepmother and stepsisters, Cinderella married the prince the very next day and went to live in the palace. The couple lived long, happy lives together, and Cinderella's stepmother and her daughters had to do their own cleaning, and never went to another ball at the palace.

The End

The Wild Swans

Far away, in a magical land, there lived a king who had eleven sons and a precious daughter, Elise. When their father remarried, the children's lives changed forever. The evil stepmother fed them sand instead of cakes and very soon sent Elise away to be brought up by peasants.

Then she cast a spell on the boys.

"Fly away in the form of great speechless birds," she cried. And, at that, the sons changed into white swans with huge flapping wings. They flew out of the windows and far away from the palace.

After many years, the king sent for his daughter. The queen was jealous of the young girl's beauty, so the queen furiously rubbed walnut juice all over her, and tangled her golden hair. When the king saw her, he cried out, "You are not my daughter!"

Elise wept, and ran far away into the forest. Lost and tired, she lay down to rest. All night she dreamed of her brothers; she missed them dearly. When she awoke, Elise bathed in a fresh pool in the forest, washing away the evil work of the queen.

Elise came across an old woman carrying a basket of berries, and asked hopefully, "Have you seen eleven princes?"

"No," the woman replied. "But yesterday I saw eleven swans with crowns on their heads swim down at the brook."

"My brothers!" Elise cried.

The old woman led Elise to the stream. There, Elise waited until at last, at sunset, she spotted eleven wild swans with golden crowns flying toward the land. When the sun disappeared, so did the swans. They transformed into the eleven princes. Elise let out a loud cry of joy as she ran to hug her brothers.

"Every morning at sunrise, we turn into swans," the eldest brother explained. "We spend the day flying and then return to our human form at sunset."

"Please come with us tomorrow, Elise," begged the youngest brother. Elise gladly agreed.

The brothers wove a mat out of willow bark to carry their sister. When morning came, they turned back into swans, and taking the mat in their beaks, they carried Elise through the sky. All day long, they flew across the empty ocean.

Finally, as night fell, they settled down in the fairy kingdom. As she slept, Elise had a dream that a fairy told her:

"Your brothers can be freed, but only if you weave eleven shirts out of stinging nettles. Until you have completed the task, you must not say a word, or else their lives will be in danger."

When Elise woke, she spent all her time weaving the shirts. The nettles stung her terribly, and before long her hands were covered with blisters, but Elise persevered.

One day as she was sewing, she looked up to find a most handsome king standing before her. When he asked her name, she was unable to speak.

Struck by her beauty, and concerned for her safety, the king reached out his hand, saying, "Come with me."

The king took her to his palace, where she was lavished with riches. But Elise could only mourn silently, and the king did not understand why. There were some in the court who were suspicious of Elise, but this did not bother the king, and he married her.

But when Elise was spotted picking nettles from the churchyard, many claimed she was a witch who wanted to destroy the kingdom.

One night as Elise crept out of the chamber, the king followed her to the eerie churchyard where he watched her pick some nettles.

"It is true. She is a witch!" he cried in despair.

The king threw Elise out of the palace, forcing her to sleep among the nettles. But this only delighted Elise, because she knew that she could now finish the shirts for her brothers.

The day came when Elise was taken in a cart to the market square, where the crowd was waiting next to a burning fire.

Suddenly, eleven wild swans surrounded her, flapping their wings in desperation. Elise had carried with her the eleven shirts and quickly threw them over the swans.

One by one they turned back into princes, but as Elise had not quite finished the last shirt, her youngest brother still had one snow-white wing.

The curse was lifted.

"Now I can speak! I am not a witch!" she cried.

Her brothers surrounded her and called out "She is innocent."

The crowd could hardly believe what they had just witnessed. They now knew this girl was not a witch.

"Forgive me," the king begged.

"Of course," Elise replied.

As the church bells rang out, and the crowd cheered, the king declared he would give each of Elise's brothers a portion of the kingdom.

They ruled wisely and with great kindness, always grateful to their devoted sister.

The End

The Little Red Hen

There was once a little red hen who lived on a farm with her friends: a sleepy cat, a lazy pig, and a stuck-up duck.

One day, the little red hen was scratching around in the farmyard when she found some grains of wheat. She was just about to peck them up when she stopped and thought.

"If I plant these grains of wheat instead of eating them," she said to herself, "they will grow tall and strong and make more wheat!" So she tucked the grains of wheat into her apron and went to see her friends.

"Who will help me plant these grains of wheat?" she asked.

The cat opened one eye.

"Not I," she said. "I'm too tired."

"Not I," snorted the pig. "It's far too hot to work."

"Not I," quacked the duck, and stood on one foot.

So the little red hen found a patch of soil. She moved the stones and dug the earth. She made a row of holes and planted all the grains of wheat. Then she watered them carefully and left them to grow.

All summer, the sun shone on the grains of wheat and the rain fell on them. Each day, the little red hen checked that they were not too dry or too wet. She pulled up the weeds and made sure the wheat had space to grow. At last, the wheat was strong and tall with fat, golden grains.

"This wheat is ready to harvest," she said to herself. "That will be a lot of work." The little red hen went to see her friends.

"I have worked all summer, and the wheat is ready. Who will help me harvest it?" she asked.

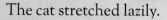

The cat stretched lazily.

"Not I," she said. "It's time for my nap."

"Not I," snorted the pig. "I need to roll in the mud."

"Not I," quacked the duck, and she preened her feathers.

So the little red hen took her tools and went to harvest the wheat. She cut down the wheat stalks and piled them up neatly. When she had finished, she went back to her friends.

"I have worked all day to cut down the wheat," she said. "Who will help me make it ready for the mill?"

The cat yawned.

"Not I," she said. "I'm sleepy."

"Not I," snorted the pig. "I'm going to lie in the sun."

"Not I," quacked the duck, and tucked her head under her wing.

So the little red hen went back to the field alone. She beat the wheat to free the grains from the stalks, and carried away the straw. The wind blew, and the little red hen worked long and hard. At last, she swept up the wheat and put it into a sack. She carried it back to her friends.

"I have worked all day to prepare the wheat," she said. "Who will help me carry it to the mill?"

"Not I," said the cat. "I need a rest."

"Not I," snorted the pig. "It looks far too heavy."

"Not I," quacked the duck, and she waddled away to the pond.

So the little red hen carried the heavy sack of wheat all the way to the mill. The kind miller ground the wheat to flour and poured it back into the sack. Then the little red hen carried it all the way home again.

The little red hen was exhausted.

"I have carried the wheat to the mill and had it ground to flour," she said. "Who will help me bake it into bread?"

"Not I," said the cat, and she curled up, ready to sleep.

"Not I," snorted the pig. "It's nearly time for my dinner."

"Not I," quacked the duck, and she sat on the ground.

So the little red hen made the flour into dough and kneaded it. She shaped it into a loaf and put it in the oven to bake. After a while, a delicious smell wafted from the kitchen. The sleepy cat opened her eyes. The lazy pig came to stand by the oven. The stuck-up duck waddled in.

At last, the bread was cooked. The little red hen carried the loaf to the table. It had a beautiful golden crust on the top and was creamy white inside. It smelled wonderful.

"Who will help me eat this loaf of bread?" the little red hen asked quietly.

"I will!" said the sleepy cat, washing her paws with her tongue.

"I will!" grunted the lazy pig, licking his lips.

"I will!" quacked the stuck-up duck, flapping her wings.

"No, you will not!" the little red hen said. "I planted the grains and watched them grow. I harvested the wheat and took it to the mill. I ground the flour and baked the bread. My chicks and I will eat the loaf!"

And that is what they did. The little red hen and her little chicks ate up every crumb of the hot, fresh bread.

The End

The Wolf in Sheep's Clothing

There was once a wolf who lived in a forest beside a sheep farm. You might think this would mean he would never be hungry, but there was a problem. Four sheepdogs guarded the large farm, and the wolf was no match for all of them.

"I should be having lamb dinner every day," whined the lean, miserable wolf. His eyes narrowed hungrily and his long red tongue drooled as he spied on the sheep from the shadows of the forest. "Look how deliciously plump they are, feeding on that lush grass all day!"

The clever sheepdogs always made sure that one of them was awake right through the night. And if that dog so much as sniffed a wolf's scent in the air, he would bark at the top of his voice until the farmer came running out.

"Stay away from my sheep!" the farmer would yell as the wolf ran for dear life back into the forest. "Come near my farm again, and it will be the end of you!"

So as the sheep grew ever fatter, the wolf became hungrier and hungrier. He didn't know how he was going to survive. Then one day, as he peered longingly through the trees, he noticed that the farmer was shearing the sheep. He watched as the thick woolly coats disappeared, one by one.

"I'm taking these to market," the farmer told his sheepdogs as he lifted the coats on to the back of his truck. "You keep an eye on that wolf for me. Any sign of him, then teach him a lesson he'll never forget."

The wolf continued to watch from the safety of the trees as the farmer drove his truck out of the farm. Just as the truck was disappearing over a hill, the wolf saw one of the bundles of wool fall off the back and on to the road. With a sly grin, the wolf suddenly had a wicked idea. Using the cover of the trees and the hedges, he sneaked along the road until he reached the bundle. He quickly unrolled it and draped the thick sheep's coat over his head and back.

"Look at me, a poor sheep who has lost his way!" he practiced his new voice. "I'd better go to that flock over there and see if they'll let me join them!"

Feeling very pleased with himself, the wolf made his way back toward the farm, being careful to keep his head near the ground.

"Baaa! Baaa!" he bleated as the four sheepdogs approached, wondering where he had come from. The wolf meekly told them his made-up story and then held his breath.

To his delight, the sheepdogs believed him and let him pass to join their flock. The sheep also believed him, taking great pity on the wolf and welcoming him right into their center. It was just where the wolf wanted to be, well hidden from the dogs.

"Are you hungry?" one of the sheep asked the wolf kindly.

"Yes, I am a little," the wolf bleated meekly, thinking how tasty the sheep looked. "I haven't eaten for days."

"Well, there's lots of lush grass here," the sheep said kindly.

The sly wolf started to plan when to pounce. He allowed himself a little smile when one sheep told him about a wolf lurking in the forest.

"Don't worry," the sheep reassured him, "the sheepdogs won't let him get anywhere near."

His cunning plan had worked. The sheep were all fooled by his sheep's coat. All, that is, except the youngest. This small, scrawny lamb kept sniffing at the wolf. She was so new to the world that she did not know what a wolf was. But she knew what a sheep was.

"She smells different than us, Mama," the lamb bleated.

"Ah, that's probably because she's had a long, rough journey," Mother explained.

"And, look, she's got claws," the lamb said, so small that she could see right underneath the wolf's false coat. "And long sharp teeth!"

At the mention of teeth, the sheep all started to bleat very loudly. The deafening noise alerted the four sheepdogs, who raced toward them. The wolf immediately broke free of the flock, his wool coat sliding off as he made desperately for the trees. The dogs were right on his heels, barking fiercely.

It was only when the wolf had reached his cave right in the middle of the forest that he knew he had escaped the dogs. But his body was still trembling from head to toe.

As for the sheep, they vowed to be a lot more careful in the future. They would never foolishly trust a stranger again, whether he looked just like them or not.

The End

Little Red Riding Hood

There was once a sweet and happy little girl whose granny had made her a lovely red cape with a hood. The little girl loved it so much that she wore it everywhere she went. Soon everyone became so used to her wearing it that they named her "Little Red Riding Hood."

"Little Red Riding Hood," said her mother one morning, "Granny is not feeling very well. Take her this basket of food and see if you can cheer her up."

Little Red Riding Hood loved to visit her granny, so she took the basket of food and set off right away.

"Go straight to Granny's house and don't talk to any strangers!" her mother called after her.

"Don't worry," sang Little Red Riding Hood as she went merrily on her way.

Little Red Riding Hood skipped off through the woods. The sun was shining, the birds were chirping in the treetops, and she didn't have a care in the world.

Very soon she met a wolf.

"Well, hello there," said the wolf in a silky, low voice. "And where are you off to on this fine morning?"

"I'm going to visit my granny," replied Little Red Riding Hood, forgetting her mother's warning. "She's not feeling well and I'm taking her this food to make her better."

The wolf licked his lips.

"Where does your dear old granny live?" asked the wolf.

"She lives in a cottage at the other side of the woods," replied Little Red Riding Hood. "It has pretty roses growing around the door."

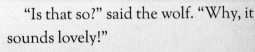

"Is that so?" said the wolf. "Why, it sounds lovely!"

There were some beautiful wild flowers growing in the woods and Little Red Riding Hood stopped to admire them.

"Why don't you pick a pretty bunch of flowers for your granny?" suggested the wolf.

Little Red Riding Hood thought that was a good idea and stooped down to pick some. As she was busy choosing the prettiest flowers, the wolf strolled away down the path. His tummy rumbled loudly. At the end of the path, he saw a cottage with roses growing around the door, just as Little Red Riding Hood had said.

The wicked old wolf knocked on the door. "Come right in, my darling," called the grandmother, thinking that it was Little Red Riding Hood.

The wolf walked into the cottage. Before the grandmother had a chance to call for help, the wicked creature opened his huge jaws and swallowed her whole! Then he climbed into her bed, pulled the covers up under his chin, and waited.

Soon, Little Red Riding Hood reached her granny's house with her basket of food and a beautiful bunch of wild flowers.

"Won't Granny be pleased to see me!" she thought, as she knocked on the door.

"Come right in, my darling," replied a strange, croaky voice.

"Poor Granny," thought Little Red Riding Hood. "She doesn't sound at all well!"

Little Red Riding Hood looked in the kitchen, but her granny wasn't there. She looked in the sitting room, but her granny wasn't there either. Finally she went into her granny's bedroom, and she gasped in surprise.

"Granny," exclaimed Little Red Riding Hood. "Your ears are absolutely enormous!"

"All the better to hear you with, my dear," replied a low, silky voice.

"And your eyes are as big as saucers," gulped Little Red Riding Hood.

"All the better to see you with," replied a rumbling, growly voice.

"And your teeth are so ... pointed!" gasped Little Red Riding Hood.

"All the better to **EAT** you with!" snarled a loud, hungry voice.

The wicked old wolf leaped out of bed and gobbled up Little Red Riding Hood in one big **GULP!** Then he lay down on the bed and fell fast asleep.

Luckily, a woodcutter was working nearby, and he heard some very loud and growly snoring sounds coming from the little cottage.

"I don't like the sound of that!" he thought. With his ax at the ready, he crept into the grandmother's house. He tiptoed into the bedroom and found the wolf fast asleep ... with his tummy bulging fit to burst!

"You wicked old wolf!"
cried the woodcutter.
"What have you done?"
He tipped the wolf
upside-down and shook
him as hard as he could.
Out fell a very dazed Little
Red Riding Hood, followed
by her poor old granny.

215

"It was so dark in there!" cried the little girl. "Thank you for saving us!"

But Little Red Riding Hood's granny was **FURIOUS!** She chased the wolf out of her bedroom, through the cottage and out into the woods. The woodcutter and Little Red Riding Hood followed close behind her.

The wolf never returned, and
Little Red Riding Hood never
spoke to strangers ever again.

The End

The Ant and the Grasshopper

Grasshopper loved the summer. He would spend all day perched on the blades of grass, basking under the sun. Just occasionally Grasshopper would hop from one blade to another, but most of the time he was happy to do absolutely nothing.

Grasshopper idly rubbed his legs together, making a happy chirping sound. "Long summer days lazing in the lush green grass," he thought to himself with a smile. "Oh, can there be anything better!"

Grasshopper was just about to doze off when there was an annoying heaving and panting sound right beneath him. It was an ant pushing a piece of corn across the ground. No wonder he was panting, because the corn was twice as big as he was, and the nearest cornfield was a good distance away.

"What a silly thing to do on a hot sunny day like this!" Grasshopper laughed. "Just look at you—all worn out!"

"It has to be done," said Ant, wiping his brow. "I have to take this corn to my nest."

"No, you don't," said Grasshopper. "You could just eat it here rather than drag it all that way. Come on, we'll have a picnic!"

Ant wiped his brow again. He would have loved to stop for a picnic, but there was far too much work to be done. "You don't understand," he told Grasshopper. "This corn isn't to eat now. It's to store in my nest," he explained.

Grasshopper laughed so much that he nearly fell off his blade of grass.

"But that means you'll be going backward and forward, heaving heavy loads, from dawn to dusk," he mocked. "In all this heat!"

"I know," said Ant. "But it's so I have plenty of food for winter. Nothing grows then. It's not like it is now, when there's food wherever you look."

Grasshopper lazily glanced all around him. It was true, there was food wherever you looked: lush grasses, golden fields of corn, delicious little fruits and berries. And it was also true that by winter it would have all disappeared. But that did not mean he was going to scurry frantically about like Ant, puffing and panting, on a hot sunny day.

"Winter's ages away," said Grasshopper. "Enjoy the lovely summer with me. Crawl up here, and let's have that picnic."

However, Ant was already crawling away, lifting the ear of corn again, heaving it across the ground.

"Crazy!" Grasshopper called after him.

"We ants like to think ahead," Ant panted in reply, not for a moment pausing in his heavy task. "Summer won't last forever."

Grasshopper jeeringly shook his head, reclining on his lush blade of grass. As he looked up at the perfect blue sky, he wondered how anyone could possibly think about winter on a day like this. It seemed to Grasshopper that summer would surely go on forever.

The summer lasted for weeks and weeks, months and months, but it did not go on forever. Eventually the long cloudless days became a little shorter. The sun was not quite so hot now, and the flowers were starting to fade. Autumn had arrived.

"I had better stock up with food," Grasshopper said to himself, climbing down from his blade of grass with a shiver. He was sure there would be a little bit left before the frost and snow arrived.

"Where can I find some food?" he asked a little mouse who was peeping out from the leaves.

"There's nothing growing," replied Mouse. "You're too late. Even the fruit that fell from the trees has all been carried away by the other animals."

Grasshopper was distraught. He felt so very hungry.

"How am I going to manage?" he asked the mouse sadly. He knew that when winter came, he would be starving.

Then he suddenly had an idea. He would visit Ant. With all that corn he had been storing up right through summer, Ant would surely have a little spare to give to his hungry friend.

By the time winter set in, the hunger and biting cold made Grasshopper weaker and weaker. It took him a long time to reach Ant's nest.

"Ant, are you there?" he called faintly. "It's your friend, Grasshopper. I've got no food. Could you spare me a little of yours?"

Ant took a good while to emerge from his nest. In fact, Grasshopper wondered whether he would appear at all. He remembered how unkind he had been to Ant in the summer.

Finally, though, Ant did emerge, and he was carrying lots of food. Grasshopper gobbled it all up gratefully. "I'm sorry I laughed at you for collecting all that corn," he said. "Next summer, I'll follow your example and think ahead!"

Ant smiled, pleased that Grasshopper had learned his lesson.

The End

The Frog Prince

There was once a princess with a smile more dazzling than the sun. She lived with her father, the king, in a palace surrounded by thick woods.

When the weather was very hot, the princess would walk into the shade of the forest and sit by a pond. There she would take out her favorite toy, a golden ball that her father had given her. Over and over, she would throw it up into the air and catch it again.

One day, the ball slipped from her hand and fell into the pond with a **SPLASH!** The pond was so deep that she couldn't see the bottom.

"My beautiful golden ball," sobbed the princess. She cried as if her heart would break, her tears drip-dropping into the water. The princess thought her favorite toy was lost forever.

An ugly, speckled frog popped his head out of the water. "Why are you crying?" he asked.

"I have dropped my precious golden ball into the water," she cried.

"What will you give me if I fetch it back for you?" asked the frog.

"You may have my jewels and pearls. Even the crown on my head," sobbed the unhappy princess.

"I don't need any of those things," said the frog. "If you promise to care for me and be my friend, let me share food from your plate and sleep on your pillow, then I will bring back your golden ball."

"I promise," said the princess, but she didn't really mean it. As the frog swam down into the murky water, she thought, "He's only a silly old frog. I won't have to do any of those things."

When the frog swam back up with the ball, she snatched it from him and ran all the way back to the palace.

That evening, the princess was having dinner with her family when there was a knock on the door.

"Princess, let me in," called a croaky voice. When the princess went to open the door, she was horrified to find the speckled frog sitting in a puddle of water. She slammed the door and hurried back to the table.

"Why do you look so frightened?" asked the king. "Was it a witch?"

"No, father, it was a frog," replied the princess.

"What does a frog want with you?" asked the puzzled king.

The princess told her father all about losing the ball and the promise she had made to the frog.

"Princesses always keep their promises, my dear," insisted the king. "Let the frog in and make him welcome."

The princess did as she was told.

As soon as the frog hopped through the door, he asked to be lifted up onto the princess's plate so that he could share her food.

When the frog saw the look of disgust on the princess's face, he sang:

*"Princess, princess, fair and sweet, you made a special vow
To be my friend and share your food, so don't forget it now."*

The king was annoyed to see his daughter acting so rudely. "This frog helped you when you were in trouble," he said. "You made him a promise, and now you must keep it."

The princess had no choice. She lifted the damp frog onto her plate and watched as he nibbled at her food.

For the rest of the evening, the frog followed the princess everywhere she went. She hoped that he would go back to his pond when it was time for bed, but he did not.

When darkness fell, the frog yawned and stretched. "I am tired," he said. "Take me to your room and let me sleep on your silken pillow."

The princess was horrified. "No, I won't!" she said. "Go back to your pond, you slimy creature, and leave me alone!"

The patient frog sang:

"Princess, princess, fair and sweet, you made a special vow
To be my friend and share your food, so don't forget it now."

The princess had no choice but to take him to her room. She couldn't bear the thought of sleeping next to him, though, so instead of placing him on her pillow, she put him in a corner on the floor. Then she climbed into her bed, laid her head down on the silken pillow, and went to sleep.

After a while, the frog jumped up onto the bed. "It's drafty on the floor. Let me sleep on your pillow as you promised," he said.

The sleepy princess felt more annoyed than ever. She picked up the frog and hurled him across the room, where he landed with a **SMACK** on the floor. The frog lay there dazed and helpless.

The princess shook herself properly awake and saw the frog lying still. She was suddenly filled with pity. She couldn't bear the thought that she might have hurt the poor thing.

"Oh, you poor darling!" she cried, and she picked him up and kissed him.

The frog transformed into a handsome young prince.

"Sweet princess," he cried. "I was bewitched, and your tender kiss has broken the curse!"

The prince and princess soon fell in love and were married. They often walked in the shady forest together and sat by the pond, tossing the golden ball back and forth, and smiling at how they first met.

The End

Dick Whittington and His Cat

Long ago there was a young orphan boy named Dick Whittington who loved to hear tales about the great city of London.

"Are the streets truly paved with gold?" he would ask, and the villagers always told him they were. So one day he decided to set off to make his fortune in London.

But as he entered the city, he found no gold. All day, he trudged through the narrow, gray streets and met people dressed in tattered clothes. Cold and hungry, Dick lay down on a doorstep and fell fast asleep.

He was woken abruptly by the bad-tempered cook of the house.

"Wake up you lazy boy," she said, prodding him, "you can't sleep here." Fortunately, Mr. Fitzwarren, a rich merchant who owned the house, took pity on the poor boy.

"Give the lad some breakfast," he told the cook. "He can work in the kitchen and sleep at the top of the house."

The cook was not pleased. She made the boy clean pots, tend the fire, and sweep the floor all day long.

Dick soon settled in, though, and the only thing he didn't like were the rats crawling all over his bed at night. So he saved up and bought himself a big cat.

In no time the cat had scared away all the rats, and she and Dick became great friends.

One day as he was busy peeling potatoes, a young girl in a beautiful silk dress appeared at the kitchen door. It was Alice, the merchant's daughter. Dick had never seen anyone looking so clean and tidy. She told Dick that her father's ship was setting sail for Africa, and it was the custom for all the servants to give the Captain of the ship a gift for good luck.

"All I have is my cat," said Dick sadly.

"Well you will just have to give that cat then," said the cook unkindly.

So the next morning Dick reluctantly handed over his cat. The cook teased him mercilessly about the cat. Dick became so unhappy, he decided to run away.

"London is not for me," he told himself.

Shortly after leaving the city behind, Dick stopped for a rest. As he sat beside a milestone, he suddenly caught the sound of the church bells. They seemed to be saying:

Turn again Whittington, Lord Mayor of London!

Dick leapt up as the pealing bells continued to ring out. He knew they were sending him a message.

"Me? Lord Mayor of London?" cried Dick. He picked up his knapsack and turned around. Then he headed straight back to the merchant's house in London.

LONDON
10 miles

Meanwhile Dick's cat had sailed all the way to Africa. The ship was met by the King, who was excited to see all the fine things brought from London. He promised the Captain gold in return for the goods and invited him to his luxurious palace for a feast.

The Captain had never seen such splendor, but soon he noticed that the palace had a problem. Rats and mice were running around freely, eating all the food.

"I think I can help you," the Captain told the King, and the next day he returned with Dick's cat. Immediately, the cat sprang into action, and in minutes all the rats and mice had scampered away.

The King had never seen a cat before and was delighted!

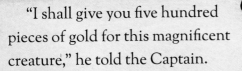

"I shall give you five hundred pieces of gold for this magnificent creature," he told the Captain.

"But if we set sail without the cat, the ship will be overrun with rats," the Captain told him. "They will eat all our food, and we will starve to death."

"A thousand pieces!" cried the King.

"The cat is yours!" replied the Captain, hoping that this was a risk worth taking.

The Captain was lucky, and the ship returned safely to London with all the gold. When Mr. Fitzwarren heard the Captain's tale, he immediately summoned Dick and told him the happy news.

"Congratulations, Mr. Whittington," he addressed Dick politely. "This gold is payment for your cat. You are a very rich man now."

And as Dick left the room, the words of the bells were in his ear:

Turn again Whittington, Lord Mayor of London!

"Maybe one day," he said to himself before setting off to buy all the servants a present. He even bought the bad-tempered cook a silver brooch. And for himself he bought fine clothes suitable for the gentleman he had now become.

Alice Fitzwarren thought he looked very handsome indeed, and soon they became sweethearts.

When Dick told Alice about the message of the bells, Alice said, "I do believe that will happen."

And she was right! Some years after Dick and Alice were married, he did indeed become Mayor of London. And occasionally, he would travel out to the milestone in his gold carriage, driven by eight beautiful white horses. There he would think about his cat and remember the first time he heard the message of the pealing bells:

Turn again Whittington, Lord Mayor of London!

The End

LONDON
10 miles

The Fir Tree

Long ago, in the middle of a forest, stood a little fir tree. All around was a wonderful smell of pine, and every day the birds sang joyfully. But the little fir tree wasn't happy.

"I wish I was big and tall like you," he complained to all the other fir trees growing high above him. "I wish I could nearly touch the sky and look out over the whole forest!"

"You will be as grand as us one day," one of the other trees chuckled. "Just be patient!"

"And enjoy being young while it lasts," said another. "It's the best time of your life."

"How can it be?" the little fir tree said to himself miserably. "I'm always in the shadows cast by the bigger trees."

Even worse for the little fir tree was the way an annoying hare kept using him for jumping practice.

"I can leap right over you," the hare gloated as he bounded up to the little fir tree and then jumped easily clear of him. It made the little fir tree so cross.

The little fir tree even envied the big trees that were chopped down by the woodcutters. The birds told him that the trees were carried on horse-drawn carriages and taken to do very important and exciting jobs. Some would become the masts of huge ships and sail around the world.

Two years went by, and the little fir tree slowly grew a bit taller. The hare could no longer jump over him now, but still the little fir tree wasn't happy.

"I wish I could be older and taller like other trees," he moaned impatiently. "Will the woodcutter ever notice me and cut me down?"

Next winter, just before Christmas, one of the woodcutters did notice the little fir tree.

"Hmm—what a fine specimen," the woodcutter said as he walked around the little fir tree. "Yes, you will be just perfect."

It hurt a little when the woodcutter swung his ax at him, but the little fir tree did not mind at all. At last, he was going to be important.

He wondered whether he was going to be made into a ship and travel the world. Instead and, just as good, he was taken to a grand house and placed in the middle of the grandest room of all with a very high ceiling. The little fir tree stood tall and proud.

Everyone in the house hurried into the room to admire the tree, and the children danced around him gleefully.

He was soon made to feel even more special when the children decorated his branches with baubles, ribbons, and twinkling lights.

How he loved to hear them giggle as they tried to place a star on the top of the tree. It felt as if he was wearing a crown.

And when they had finished, the children joined the adults in singing songs they called "Christmas carols."

At the end of the evening, before turning off the lights, the mother took one last look at the little fir tree.

"Beautiful!" she said. "Surely the finest Christmas tree ever!"

The little fir tree had never felt so proud.

Early the next morning, the children rushed in to see him. He thought they were going to dance around him again, but this time they just grabbed the boxes from under the tree and ripped off the pretty paper.

The very next day, the little fir tree was shocked to hear the servants say, "Time to take this old tree down."

After all the decorations had been removed, the little fir tree was carried up into the cold, dark loft. All he had for company were a few mice, sheltering from the snow outside.

To pass the time, the little fir tree would tell the mice stories about his forest days—the warm shafts of sunlight, the wonderful tickling breezes, and the chattering birds.

He even smiled when telling them about the annoying hare always jumping over him.

"It was actually a lot of fun," he admitted.

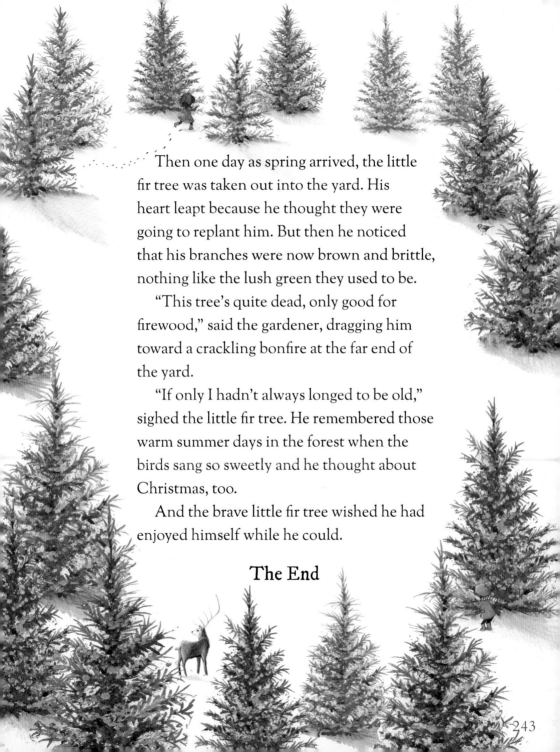

Then one day as spring arrived, the little fir tree was taken out into the yard. His heart leapt because he thought they were going to replant him. But then he noticed that his branches were now brown and brittle, nothing like the lush green they used to be.

"This tree's quite dead, only good for firewood," said the gardener, dragging him toward a crackling bonfire at the far end of the yard.

"If only I hadn't always longed to be old," sighed the little fir tree. He remembered those warm summer days in the forest when the birds sang so sweetly and he thought about Christmas, too.

And the brave little fir tree wished he had enjoyed himself while he could.

The End

The Little Mermaid

Long, long ago, a mer-king lived under the sea with his six mermaid daughters, who all had long wavy hair and sang with sweet heavenly voices.

The mermaids loved their watery world, but they liked to hear the wise sea king tell them stories about the world above the sea.

"Oh, father, tell us about the cities and the trees and flowers!" they would cry.

"When you are twenty-one, my little ones," their father would say, "you can go to the surface and see all these wonders for yourself."

One by one, the sisters got their chance to visit the surface. At last it was the turn of the youngest sister. The little mermaid swam up through the crystal waters to the ocean surface with great joy in her heart.

Close by was a big
ship. She could see
people on the deck throwing a
party for the prince who was on board.

The little mermaid couldn't keep her eyes off the handsome prince.
As she swam closer for a better look, the sea started to swell and a
strong wind whipped up.

"Oh no!" cried the little mermaid. "A storm is coming."

Suddenly, as the ship was tossed from side to side, the prince was
thrown into the churning water. He began to sink beneath the waves
and would have drowned had the little mermaid not dived down to
rescue him.

Swimming close to the land, she gently pushed the unconscious
prince onto the beach. His eyes flickered open for a few seconds, and
he smiled before closing them again. As she swam away, she glanced
back at the shore. A group of people had gathered around the prince.
They helped him to his feet and led him away down the beach.

The little mermaid dived beneath the waves and swam back home.

The little mermaid longed to see the prince again. She became so sad that eventually she told her sisters about the prince and how she had fallen in love with him.

"I know where his palace is," said her oldest sister. "I'll show you."

After that, the little mermaid swam to the surface every day. She gazed at the palace hoping to catch a glimpse of the prince.

"Father, could I become human, if I wanted to?" she asked the king one day.

"The only way, my little one," said the king gently, "is if a human falls in love with you."

But the little mermaid could not forget the prince. She decided to visit the sea witch.

"I can make a potion to make you human," hissed the witch. "But I will take your beautiful voice as my payment. If you win the true love of the prince, only then will you get your voice back."

The little mermaid loved the prince so much that she agreed. She swam to the prince's palace and drank the potion. She fell into a deep sleep.

When she woke up, she was lying on the beach dressed in beautiful clothes. Where her shiny tail had been, she now had a pair of pale human legs. The little mermaid tried to stand, but her new legs wobbled and she stumbled on the sand.

As she fell, two strong arms reached out and caught her. The little mermaid looked up. It was the prince! She tried to speak but her voice had gone, and she could only smile at her handsome rescuer.

The silent, beautiful, and mysterious stranger fascinated the prince. He grew very fond of the little mermaid and spent his afternoons with her around the palace and on the beach.

One day, the prince told the little mermaid that he was getting married to a princess.

"My parents want me to do this," he sighed sadly. "But I love another girl. I don't know who she is, but she once rescued me from the sea."

The little mermaid was devastated, but without a voice, how could she tell the prince that she was that girl?

The prince now took walks along the beach with the princess. The little mermaid could do nothing but watch on from afar.

Over time, the little mermaid became more and more jealous as she saw the prince smiling and laughing. But, deep down, she knew his heart didn't belong to the princess.

A few days before the wedding, the prince asked the little mermaid to take a walk with him along the beach.

"Once I'm married, I won't be able to spend any time with you," he told her.

The little mermaid nodded sadly. She had been dreading this happening.

As they walked across the sand, a fierce wind suddenly whipped along the shore. A huge wave crashed over the prince and the little mermaid, washing them out to sea. Without thinking, the little mermaid dived beneath the churning waves and grabbed the prince.

As the prince lay coughing and spluttering on the sand, he stared at the little mermaid.

"You're the girl who saved me before!" he cried. "I remember now."

The little mermaid smiled and nodded.

"I can't marry the princess. I love you," he sighed. "I don't care if you can't speak. Will you marry me?"

The little mermaid had never felt so joyful and, as the prince kissed her, something magical happened. She could feel her voice returning! Bubbling with excitement, she cried out, "Yes, I will marry you!"

The happy couple were married the very next day. The little mermaid's dreams had come true, but she never forgot her family, or that she had once been a mermaid.

The End

The Lion and the Mouse

Once upon a time, there was a huge lion who lived in a dark, rocky den in the middle of the jungle. When the lion wasn't out hunting, he loved to curl up in his den and sleep. In fact, as his friends knew, if he didn't get enough sleep, the lion became extremely grumpy.

One day, while the lion lay sleeping as usual, a little mouse thought he'd take a short cut straight through the lion's den. The mouse lived with his family in a hollow at the bottom of a tall tree just on the other side of the lion's rocky home. He was on his way home for supper and didn't want to have to climb up and over the big boulders surrounding the den.

"What harm can it do?" he thought. "He's snoring so loudly, he'll never hear me."

As he hurried past the snoring beast, he accidentally ran over the lion's paw. With a mighty roar, the lion woke up and grabbed the little mouse in one quick motion.

"How dare you wake me up!" the lion roared angrily. "Don't you know who I am? I am King of the Beasts! No one disturbs my sleep. I will kill you and eat you for my supper." He opened his huge mouth wide.

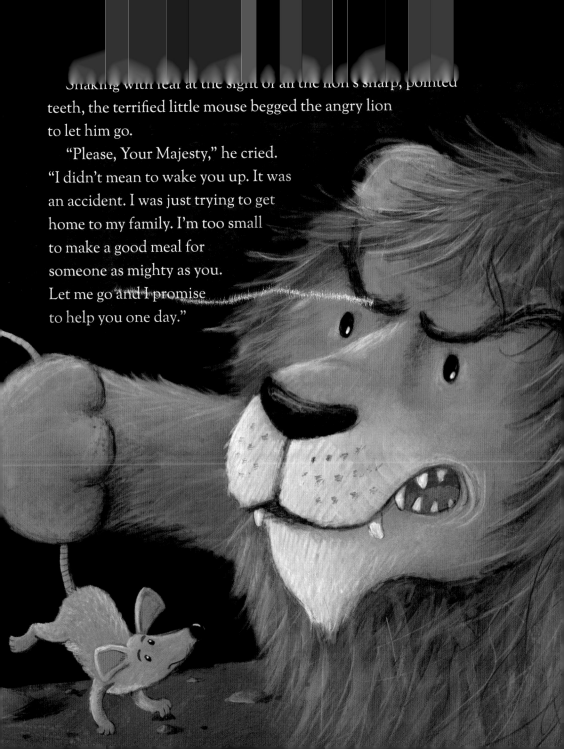

Shaking with fear at the sight of all the lion's sharp, pointed teeth, the terrified little mouse begged the angry lion to let him go.

"Please, Your Majesty," he cried. "I didn't mean to wake you up. It was an accident. I was just trying to get home to my family. I'm too small to make a good meal for someone as mighty as you. Let me go and I promise to help you one day."

The grumpy lion stared at the little mouse. Then he laughed loudly.

"You help me?" he said scornfully, shaking his furry mane. "Ha! Ha! Ha! What a ridiculous idea! You're too small to help someone as big as me."

The little mouse trembled and closed his eyes as he waited for the terrible jaws to snap him up.

But to his surprise, the lion didn't eat him. Instead, the lion smiled and opened his paw.

"Go home, little mouse," said the lion. "You have made me laugh and put me in a good mood, so I will let you go. But hurry, before I change my mind."

The little mouse was very grateful. "Thank you, Your Majesty!" he squeaked. "I promise to be your friend forever, and I won't disturb you again."

As quickly as he could, the little mouse scurried home. What a story he would have to tell his children!

A few days later, the lion was out hunting in the jungle. As he crept stealthily through the lush undergrowth, he smelled something delicious. There, in a small clearing just ahead of him, stood a goat, eating the grass beneath a shady tree.

The lion circled the clearing, slowly crawling through the tall grass. He crouched low, ready to pounce on the unsuspecting goat ... when suddenly a big net fell on him.

He was trapped in a hunter's snare!

The goat, bleating in terror, ran off into the jungle. The lion roared and tried to break free from the trap. But the more he struggled, the more he became tangled in the net. He was so angry that he let out the loudest of roars.

RROOAARR!

The trees in the jungle shook with the terrible noise. Every animal for miles heard it, including the little mouse.

"Oh no!" squeaked the mouse. "That's my friend, the lion. He must be in trouble! I've got to go and help him."

"Be careful, my dear," cried the mouse's wife. "Remember how big he is!"

The little mouse scurried through the jungle as fast as his tiny legs would carry him, toward the lion's mighty roar.

Soon he came upon the clearing and the lion, tangled and trapped in the ropes of the hunter's net.

"Keep still, Your Majesty," cried the mouse. "I'll have you out of there in no time."

"You?" laughed the lion.

The mouse ignored him and quickly started gnawing through the net with his sharp little teeth.

Before long, there was a big hole in the net, and the lion squeezed through the ropes and escaped his trap.

The lion held out his giant paw toward the little mouse. "Thank you, my little friend," he said humbly, bowing his huge head. "I was wrong when I laughed at you and said that someone as small as you couldn't help me. You saved my life today, and I am truly grateful."

The little mouse smiled up at the lion. "You were kind enough to let me go before, and I promised I would pay you back one day," he squeaked. "It was my turn to help you."

Side by side, the big lion and little mouse walked back into the jungle. From that day on the huge, mighty lion and the tiny, mighty mouse became the best of friends.

The End

How the Camel Got His Hump

Long ago when the earth was still new, all the animals worked hard for their friend, Man. The horse carried Man on his back, the dog fetched wood for him, and the ox plowed the fields. But the lazy camel stayed in the desert and refused to do any work. He spent his time staring at his reflection in a pool of water, admiring his lovely slender neck and very long legs. The camel was always very unfriendly and only had one thing to say to the other animals: **"Humph!"**

One day, the horse rode deep into the desert and said to the camel, "Come out and trot with us."

"**Humph!**" replied the camel.

The next to approach the lazy creature was the dog. He came bounding up with a stick in his mouth. Excitedly, he dropped the stick and said, "Camel, come and fetch and carry like the rest of us."

"**Humph!**" came the reply as the camel continued to stare at his reflection.

When the ox heard how rude the camel had been, he decided to try. He trudged through the hot desert and finally reached the lazy camel.

"Come and help us plow," he said.

But the only response was "**Humph!**" Camel was in no mood to talk to anyone.

At the end of the day, the Man called the three animals together.

"That lazy camel in the desert refuses to do any work," he said. "Now you will all have to work double time."

The three animals were very angry. They held a pow-wow to discuss what could be done.

"We can't go on working like this," complained the horse. And they all agreed.

Presently the Djinn of all Deserts appeared in a whoosh and a swoosh, rolling in a cloud of dust. Now the Djinn was a magic creature who always traveled that way. He was in charge of all deserts and was very wise.

"Oh, Djinn of all Deserts, is it right for anyone to be idle, with the world being so new?" asked the horse.

"Certainly not," replied the Djinn.

"Well," said the horse, "there's a thing in the middle of the desert with a long neck, long legs, and a flat back. He hasn't done a stroke of work for three days."

"What does he say about it?" asked the Djinn.

"He only says, **'Humph!'**" said the dog. "And he won't fetch and carry."

"Does he say anything else?" asked the Djinn.

"No, and he refuses to plow," added the ox.

"Then I shall need to pay this lazy creature a visit," the Djinn of all Deserts told the three tired animals.

The very next day the camel was, as usual, admiring himself. Suddenly there was a whoosh and a swoosh, and clouds of sand rose high into the air. Camel thought it was a sandstorm until the Djinn of all Deserts landed with a thump at his feet.

"Humph!" said the camel, although secretly he was very interested in the magical vision before him.

"What is all this I hear?" asked the Djinn. "Why are you not working, with the world being so new?"

"Humph!" replied the camel.

"You have given the horse, the dog, and the ox a lot of extra work on account of your laziness. Aren't you a little sorry?"

"Humph!" came the same reply.

"Use that word once more and you will be sorry," warned the Djinn.

"Humph!" said the camel, but this was to be once too often.

The Djinn of all Deserts sat with his chin in his hand and began to work a great magic. Soon the perfectly flat back of the camel began to puff up and up into a great big lolloping humph.

"What has happened to my beautiful flat back?" cried the camel, with huge salty tears falling onto the dry sand.

"Now you have your very own humph," the Djinn told him. "You brought this on yourself by your laziness." The camel was startled by this outburst. "Now you are going to put that humph to work," continued the Djinn.

"But how can I work with this huge humph on my back?" the camel quickly replied.

"It's the humph that will help you work," the Djinn told him. "That humph will hold three days' food. You owe everyone three days' work, so now you can work and not have to stop to eat."

The camel drooped his head sadly.

"And there will be no time to admire your reflection in the water," the Djinn of all Deserts added. And with a whoosh and a swoosh, he flew into the air.

And so the camel and his humph went to join the horse, the dog, and the ox. And from that day to this, the camel always wears a humph (which we call hump now, not to hurt his feelings). But he has never yet made up those three days that he missed at the beginning of the world, and he has never yet learned how to behave.

The End

The Princess and the Pea

Once upon a time, in a kingdom far away, there lived a handsome prince. He had loving parents, plenty of friends, and lived a wonderful life in his castle. But one thing made him sad. He did not have a wife.

The prince had always wanted to marry a princess. But he wanted her to be clever and funny, and loving and kind. None of the princesses that he met at parties and balls were quite right.

Some of the princesses were too mean, some were too rude. Some were too quiet, some were too loud.

And some were just plain boring!

So, the prince decided to travel the world in the hope of finding a perfect princess. He met many more princesses who tried to impress him with their beauty, their dancing, and their baking ... but still none were quite right.

"I'm never going to meet the right princess," he sighed to himself. "Oh, where is that girl of my dreams?"

Months passed without success, so eventually the prince headed back to his castle.

"Cheer up, my son," said the king. "You are still young. One day you will meet a wonderful girl, just like I met your mother." The king smiled at the queen, but he was at a loss to know how to make the prince happy again.

Then one night, when even the king and queen had begun to give up hope of their son ever finding a bride, there was a terrible storm. Thunder roared, lightning flashed, and the rain poured down.

Suddenly there was a loud knock on the wooden castle door.

"I wonder who could be out on such a terrible stormy night?" said the prince. When he opened the door, a pretty young girl stared back at him. She was soaked from head to toe.

"Oh please, Your Royal Highness, may I come in for a moment?" she pleaded. "I was traveling to see some friends, but I got lost in this storm, and now I am very cold and very wet."

The prince ushered the poor girl in out of the wind and the rain.

"You poor thing," said the queen. "You must stay the night. You cannot travel on in this weather."

The prince smiled at the girl. "What is your name?" he asked her.

"I'm Princess Penelope," she replied. "You are all very kind. I don't want to be a bother to you."

At the word princess, the queen smiled to herself. "I wonder ..." she thought, but she didn't say anything. She took the girl's hand and said aloud, "Of course not, my dear. Come, and let's get you warm."

Once the princess had changed into some dry clothes, the queen invited her to have some supper with the family.

The prince listened contentedly as the charming princess chatted away over their meal. He could not stop gazing at her. She was clever and funny, and loving and kind. By the end of the evening the prince had fallen in love!

The queen was delighted when she saw what was happening, but she wanted to be quite sure that Princess Penelope was a real princess. She went to the guest room in the castle and placed a tiny pea under the mattress. Then she told the servants to pile twenty more mattresses onto the bed. Then the queen had twenty feather quilts piled on top of the twenty mattresses!

"Now we shall see if you are a real princess!" murmured the queen to herself.

The queen showed the princess to her room and tucked her into the towering bed. "Sleep well, my dear," she said.

In the morning the princess came down to breakfast, rubbing her eyes.

"How did you sleep, my dear?" the queen asked her.

The princess didn't want to be rude, but she couldn't lie. "I'm afraid I hardly slept a wink!" she replied, stifling a yawn.

"I'm so sorry, my dear," said the queen. "Was the bed not comfortable?"

"There were so many lovely mattresses and quilts, it should have been very comfortable," replied the princess, "but I could feel something lumpy and bumpy, and now I am black and blue all over!"

The queen grinned and hugged the girl to her. "That proves it," cried the queen. "Only a real princess would be able to feel a tiny pea through twenty mattresses and twenty feather quilts!"

The prince was filled with joy. He had finally met the princess of his dreams!

Not long after that, the prince asked Princess Penelope to be his wife. She happily agreed, and they were married in the castle.

The prince was never unhappy again. And as for the pea, it was put in the royal museum as proof that perfect princesses do exist!

The End

The Peacock and the Crane

There was once a king in a far-off land who had a magnificent palace. But his pride and joy were his stunning gardens, full of exotic trees and hedges, pretty fountains and quaint little mazes. Roaming around the palace gardens were graceful deer, while majestic swans and beautiful ducks drifted on its lakes.

But of all the animals that lived in the palace gardens, surely the most glorious was the king's peacock. Unfortunately, the peacock knew this, too.

"Hello, deer," the peacock greeted them as he strutted across the grass, dragging his long tail feathers behind him.

"Hello, Peacock," the deer replied, knowing what question was going to come next.

"Who do you think is the most beautiful creature in the king's gardens?" the peacock asked, holding high his silvery blue neck and making his crown feathers stand up proudly on his head.

Now, the deer were themselves beautiful creatures, with huge eyes and pretty spots, but they simply could not compare to the peacock.

"You are the most beautiful, Peacock," the deer all replied humbly.

"Just as I thought!" said the peacock, and he swept off to find another creature so he could ask exactly the same question.

The swans gliding gracefully across the lake were also very beautiful, with proud necks and pure white feathers gleaming in the sun. The same was true of the ducks. The king had specially chosen this exotic breed with orange tail feathers, and a lovely blush on their cheeks.

But, again, they could not compare to the peacock.

"You are the most beautiful, Peacock," the swans and ducks all admitted as the peacock asked the same question of each and every one of them.

Peacock smiled as he strutted around the palace gardens. How he loved to hear that answer. If any of the other animals hesitated for a moment, the peacock would quickly convince them by his favorite trick. He would suddenly raise his tail feathers to produce a huge, magnificent fan covered with shimmering blue and green spots. Faced with this stunning display, how could anyone deny that he was the most beautiful creature of all?

One day, Peacock noticed that the king had added a new animal to the palace gardens. It was a large wading bird, standing meekly at the edge of the lake. The peacock scoffed at the sight of this new arrival. It was the plainest creature he had ever seen, with dull gray feathers and lanky legs.

"What are you?" asked the peacock as he swept gracefully up to the gray newcomer.

"I'm a crane," the other replied.

"Is that so?" asked the peacock, rudely looking him up and down. "Are you proud of being a crane?"

"Oh yes," he replied confidently.

This annoyed Peacock. How could anyone looking as dull as that be so proud? Right away, the peacock asked his usual question.

"Who do you think is the most beautiful creature in the palace gardens?"

"Mm, I'm not sure," said the crane. "I haven't met everyone yet."

The peacock was more annoyed than ever. How was this dull creature likely to meet someone more beautiful than him? So, he did his usual trick—only this time he not only raised his tail feathers to produce a glorious blue and green fan, he also slowly turned this magnificent fan to the left and right.

"Now, who do you think is the most beautiful creature in the palace gardens?" the peacock taunted.

The crane was dazzled by the magnificent sight before him.

"It would surely be you," the crane said.

"At last! You've finally opened your eyes!" jeered the peacock.

"But beauty isn't everything," added the crane.

"What?" screeched the peacock in disbelief. "You mean, you don't want to look like me? You would rather be a plain, dull crane?"

"Yes, my feathers are rather plain and dull," the crane admitted. "But they serve me well, giving me a lot of pleasure." And to demonstrate, the crane opened his wings and took gracefully to the air. He flew all around the palace gardens, high above them.

"You see, your feathers might be beautiful," the crane called down, "but that's all they are, just for show. They can't make you fly and see all the wonderful things I can see."

The peacock enviously watched the crane circling high above, as happy as could be. That dull, gray bird was right: beauty isn't everything, and there are a lot of other things that are important, too. Peacock decided that he would never boast again.

The End

Chicken Little

One day, Chicken Little was walking along when an acorn fell from a tree and bounced off his head. The acorn rolled away before Chicken Little knew what had hit him.

"Oh, my! Oh, dear!" he clucked. "Whatever shall I do?"

Chicken Little flew into a panic. He ran around in circles in a flap, losing feathers as he went.

Along came Henny Penny.

"What's the matter?" she asked.

"THE SKY IS FALLING! THE SKY IS FALLING!" cried Chicken Little, still in a panic.

Henny Penny was shocked. She did not know such a thing could happen.

"Cluck-a-cluck-cluck!" she shrieked. "We must tell the king at once!"

So Chicken Little and Henny Penny rushed off to tell the king.

They flapped down the road, clucking as they went. Soon they met Cocky Locky.

"Where are you going in such a hurry?" he asked.

"THE SKY IS FALLING! THE SKY IS FALLING!" cried Chicken Little.

"We're off to tell the king!" chattered Henny Penny.

Cocky Locky gasped. It would be terrible if the sky fell.

"Cock-a-doodle-doo," crowed Cocky Locky. "I'll come with you!"

So Chicken Little, Henny Penny, and Cocky Locky rushed off to tell the king.

They flapped and they flustered down the road, clucking and crowing as they went. Soon they met Ducky Lucky.

"Why are you flapping so?" she asked.

"THE SKY IS FALLING! THE SKY IS FALLING!" cried Chicken Little.

"We're off to tell the king!" crowed Cocky Locky.

Ducky Lucky frowned. She didn't like the sound of that.

"How w-w-worrying," she quacked nervously. "I'm c-c-coming with you."

So Chicken Little, Henny Penny, Cocky Locky, and Ducky Lucky rushed off to tell the king.

They flapped and they flustered and they fidgeted down the road, clucking and crowing and quacking as they went. Soon they met Drakey Lakey.

"What's all the fuss about?" he asked.

"THE SKY IS FALLING! THE SKY IS FALLING!" cried Chicken Little.

"We're off to tell the king!" quacked Ducky Lucky.

Drakey Lakey was dumbfounded. He dreaded the thought of a falling sky.

"Darn it!" he squawked. "I'll join you on your journey!"
So Chicken Little, Henny Penny, Cocky Locky, Ducky
Lucky, and Drakey Lakey rushed off to tell the king.

They flapped and they flustered and they fidgeted and they flurried down the road, clucking and crowing and quacking and squawking as they went. Soon they met Goosey Loosey.

"What's ruffled your feathers?" she asked.

"THE SKY IS FALLING! THE SKY IS FALLING!" cried Chicken Little.

"We're off to tell the king!" squawked Drakey Lakey.

Goosey Loosey shuddered. Could it really be true?

"How horrible!" she honked. "I'm coming with you."

So Chicken Little, Henny Penny, Cocky Locky, Ducky Lucky, Drakey Lakey, and Goosey Loosey rushed off to tell the king.

They flapped and they flustered and they fidgeted and they flurried and they flopped down the road, clucking and crowing and quacking and squawking and honking as they went. Soon they met Turkey Lurkey.

"Where are you waddling to?" she asked.

"THE SKY IS FALLING! THE SKY IS FALLING!" cried Chicken Little.

"We're off to tell the king!" honked Goosey Loosey.

Turkey Lurkey trembled. She thought that sounded truly terrible!

"My goodness!" she gobbled. "I'm coming with you!"

So Chicken Little, Henny Penny, Cocky Locky, Ducky Lucky, Drakey Lakey, Goosey Loosey, and Turkey Lurkey rushed off to tell the king.

They flapped and they flustered and they fidgeted and they flurried and they flopped and they floundered down the road, clucking and crowing and quacking and squawking and honking and gobbling as they went. Soon they met Foxy Loxy.

"Well, hello!" he said. "Why are you all in such a tizzy?"

"THE SKY IS FALLING! THE SKY IS FALLING!" cried Chicken Little.

"We're off to tell the king!" gobbled Turkey Lurkey.

Foxy Loxy smiled slyly. He had never seen so many plump birds in such a fearsome flap.

"Well I never," soothed Foxy Loxy. "Don't worry, I know the quickest way to reach the king. Follow me."

So Chicken Little, Henny Penny, Cocky Locky, Ducky Lucky, Drakey Lakey, Goosey Loosey, and Turkey Lurkey followed Foxy Loxy down a long path and into some dark woods.

"Not far to go now," said Foxy Loxy.

They lumbered over logs and they lolloped over leaves until they found themselves at ... Foxy Loxy's den!

Foxy Loxy and all his family licked their lips.

"Run!" cried Chicken Little.

"Fly!" shrieked Henny Penny.

"Hurry!" honked Goosey Loosey.

And Chicken Little, Henny Penny, Cocky Locky, Ducky Lucky, Drakey Lakey, Goosey Loosey, and Turkey Lurkey ran as fast as their legs could carry them.

They flapped and they flustered and they fidgeted and they flurried and they flopped and they floundered right out of the woods and back up the long path, clucking and crowing and quacking and squawking and honking and gobbling as they went.

And they never did tell the king about the sky falling.

The End

The Musicians of Bremen

There was once a donkey who worked tirelessly carrying sacks to the mill. After many years, the donkey grew weak and his master considered giving him away. One day the donkey decided to run away, setting forth on the road to Bremen.

"I can be the town musician and make a new life for myself," he said excitedly.

When he had gone a little way, he found a dog lying in the road, panting and howling.

"Why are you so short of breath?" the donkey asked kindly.

"Ah," replied the dog. "I am old and getting weaker everyday. I cannot hunt anymore, and my master has no use for me, so I left him. But what am I going to do now?"

"I am on my way to Bremen to be the town musician," the donkey told him enthusiastically. "Why don't you come with me?"

The dog happily agreed.

Soon they came across a cat with a face as long
as three rainy days.

"Why the sad face, Old Whiskers?" asked
the donkey.

"How can I be cheerful?" replied the old cat.
"I would rather sit by the stove and purr than chase
around after mice. My mistress has little use for me.
But where should I go?"

"Come with us to Bremen," the donkey told him.
"We can make fine music in the town."

The cat quickly agreed.

Soon the three runaways reached a farmyard where the rooster was sitting on a gate crying out, **"Cock-a-doodle-doo!"**

"Whatever is the matter?" asked the donkey.

"The farmer's wife is going to cook me for supper!" he told them. "So I want to sing while I still can."

"Listen, my red-headed bird," said the donkey. "Join us on our journey to Bremen. You have a pleasing voice, and together we can make good music there."

The rooster thought this was a splendid plan.

So the donkey, the dog, the cat, and the rooster all set off for the town of Bremen. But they could not reach there in one day.

As evening fell they agreed to spend the night in the forest. The four friends found it difficult to sleep.

"There's a house not too far away," the rooster called out as he spotted a little spark in the distance.

"Then we must go, as there is little comfort here," the donkey said.

"I could do well with a few bones with a little meat on them," agreed the dog, licking his lips.

And soon the four travelers were standing in front of a large house. The donkey, as the biggest, went toward the window.

"What do you see, gray-horse?" asked the rooster.

"Ah," answered the donkey, "I see a table set with good things to eat and drink. There are sparkling jewels and gold piled high." He paused before adding, "And I see robbers, too!"

So the friends planned to drive the thieves away.

The donkey stood with his front feet on the window. The dog then jumped on the donkey's back, and the cat climbed on top of the dog. Finally the rooster flew up and sat on the cat's head. And when the four musicians were in place, the donkey called out, "Now, we must sing for our supper."

So the donkey brayed, the dog barked, the cat meowed, and the rooster cock-a-doodle-dooed. Then they all burst through the shutters.

Thinking there was a ghost, the robbers jumped up, screaming, and fled into the woods.

After eating the leftovers, the exhausted friends soon fell asleep.

At midnight one of the robbers crept back into the house. First, he went into the kitchen, but it was so dark he didn't see the cat lying on the hearth. He made the mistake of thinking the cat's fiery eyes were live coals and tried to strike a match in front of them. The startled cat jumped up, spitting and scratching him. Then, as the frightened robber ran toward the door, he tripped over the dog, who leapt up and bit him in the leg.

And his misery did not end there. Just as he was fleeing across the yard, he stumbled and fell on top of the donkey, who kicked out in his sleep.

Hearing all the commotion, the rooster woke up with a lively, **"Cock-a-doodle-doo!"**

The terrified robber ran for his life. He was still trembling when he finally reached his friends.

"There is a horrible witch sitting in the house," he told them breathlessly. "She scratched my face with her long fingers. And there is a man standing at the door, and he jabbed me in the leg. And a black monster is lying in the yard, and it struck me with a wooden club. And there's a judge sitting up on the roof calling out, 'Bring the rascal here.'"

And from that time, the robbers never returned to the house. But the four musicians of Bremen liked it so much, they never left again.

The End

The Three Billy Goats Gruff

Once upon a time, there were three goats—a little white one, a medium-sized brown one, and a big gray one.
They were the Billy Goats Gruff, and they were brothers.
The little Billy Goat Gruff had little horns.
The medium-sized Billy Goat Gruff had medium-sized horns.
And the big Billy Goat Gruff had big, curly horns!

The three brothers lived in a small meadow beside a river. All day long they ate the green grass.

On the other side of the river, over a rickety wooden bridge, was a huge field. The Billy Goats Gruff thought the grass there looked longer and greener and juicier!

Day after day, the three Billy Goats Gruff looked longingly at the juicy grass on the other side of the river. They would have happily crossed the bridge to go there, but for one thing.

One horrible thing.

A mean and smelly old troll with very pointy teeth lived under the bridge, and he guarded it day and night.

The grass in the meadow where the three Billy Goats Gruff lived got shorter and shorter, and drier and browner, and the brothers were getting hungrier and hungrier for fresh, juicy grass.

One day, the little Billy Goat Gruff decided he'd had enough.

"I'm so hungry!" he cried to his brothers. "I can't eat one more blade of this dry, brown grass."

"We agree!" groaned his two brothers. "Look at that juicy grass over there. Oh, if only we could get past the mean old troll."

"I'm going to try," said the little Billy Goat Gruff bravely. And off he set, **TRIP TRAP, TRIP TRAP,** across the bridge.

Suddenly a croaky voice roared out, "Who's that **TRIP TRAPPING** over my bridge? I'll eat you if you pass. You'd taste yummy in a sandwich!"

"Oh, please don't eat me," cried the little goat. He was very frightened, but he had a plan. "I'm only a little goat. My brother will be crossing in a minute, and he is much bigger and tastier than me!"

The greedy troll thought about this and burped loudly. "All right," he said, "you may cross."

The little Billy Goat Gruff ran as fast as his little legs would take him until he reached the other side.

The medium-sized goat saw his little brother munching the juicy grass on the other side of the river. He really wanted to eat that grass, too.

He turned to the big Billy Goat Gruff. "If he can cross the bridge, then so can I!" he said. And off he set, **TRIP TRAP, TRIP TRAP,** across the bridge.

Suddenly, the mean troll climbed out from his hiding place.

"Who's that **TRIP TRAPPING** over my bridge? I'll eat you if you pass. You'd taste nice with rice!" He licked his lips when he noticed how much bigger this goat was.

The medium-sized Billy Goat Gruff stopped, his hooves clacking together in fear.

"Oh, please don't eat me," he cried. "I'm really not that big. My brother will be crossing in a minute, and he is so much bigger and tastier than me!"

The troll rolled his eyes, licked dribble from his chin, and grunted that the medium-sized goat could cross the bridge.

The medium-sized Billy Goat Gruff galloped quickly across the bridge to join his little brother, before the mean troll changed his mind.

The big Billy Goat Gruff had been watching his brothers.

"I'm big and strong ... and I'm really hungry!" he said to himself. So off he set, **TRIP TRAP, TRIP TRAP**, across the bridge to join his brothers and eat the juicy green grass on the other side.

As before, the mean, smelly troll scrabbled up onto the bridge.

"Who's that **TRIP TRAPPING** over my bridge? I'll eat you if you pass. You'd taste scrumptious in a stew!" This goat was big! The troll's mouth started watering, and his large tummy started rumbling.

The big Billy Goat Gruff stamped his hooves. "No, you can't eat me!" he shouted. "I'm big and I have big horns, and I will toss you into the river if you don't let me pass."

Before the troll could answer, the big Billy Goat Gruff put his head down and charged at him. He tossed the mean creature high up into the air.

Down,
down,
down

fell the troll. With a huge splash, he dropped into the river and floated away. And that was the end of the mean troll.

"Maaaa! Well done, big brother!" laughed the little Billy Goat Gruff and the medium-sized Billy Goat Gruff. "Come and eat this grass—it is truly juicy and delicious!"

And the three Billy Goats Gruff were never hungry again.

The End

Snow-White and Rose-Red

There was once a poor widow who had two daughters, Snow-White and Rose-Red. In her little garden grew two rose trees—one with white roses and the other with red. The two sisters played in the forest in summer, and on winter evenings they would listen to their mother's tales as she sat at her spinning wheel.

One snowy evening there was a loud rapping at the door.

"Hurry," called their mother, "it must be a traveler who is lost." But when Rose-Red opened the door, she screamed as she saw a huge great brown bear panting loudly.

"Please do not be afraid," growled the bear. "I'm half frozen, and I merely want to warm up."

Immediately, the kind mother ushered the bear in and let him lie by the fire. At first the sisters were wary of the huge creature, but by the end of the evening they were playing happily with him.

For the rest of winter, the bear came every evening and the sisters loved to spend time with him. When spring came, they were very sad when the bear told them, "The dwarfs will soon be back, so I must go deep into the forest to stop them from taking my treasure." And he thanked the mother and sisters for their kindness.

As the days grew warmer and longer and the red and white roses bloomed once more, the sisters spent their time playing in the forest. On one hot afternoon, they stumbled across a very cross-looking dwarf. One end of his long white beard was trapped under a heavy log, and he was waving his arms frantically.

"Well, do something to help!" he snapped.

The sisters rushed to his side but couldn't shift the log, so Snow-White took out her scissors and cut off the end of his beard. The dwarf was not pleased. Snatching up a bag of gold that he had dropped, he pushed past shouting, "Bad luck to you both!"

Later, when the girls were playing by the stream, they were startled by something jumping in the air. They thought it was a grasshopper, but it was the old dwarf. He was caught on a fishing line and his beard was entangled in the thin wire. So once again Snow-White and Rose-Red tried to help, and this time it was Rose-Red who snipped his beard to free him. And once again the bad-tempered dwarf grumbled. He snatched a sack of pearls that were hidden in the reeds and ran off.

Later that afternoon, the mother sent the two sisters to the town to buy needles and thread, and laces and ribbons. Crossing the heath, they noticed a large bird hovering in the air. As it sank lower and lower, they heard a piercing cry. To their horror, the sisters saw that the eagle had seized the old dwarf.

Taking pity, the two girls grabbed hold of the little man tightly. As they pulled him from the claws of the eagle, the ungrateful dwarf complained, "You've torn my coat, you clumsy creatures." Then he quickly grabbed a sack of precious stones and ran off toward the woods as fast as his little legs would take him.

By this time, the girls were used to his ingratitude and continued on their way into town.

As they crossed the heath again on their way home, Snow-White and Rose-Red spotted the old dwarf sitting cross-legged in the meadow. He was counting all his treasure. Seeing the exquisite stones glisten in the sun, the sisters couldn't help but gasp at their beauty.

"How dare you sneak up on me!" shouted the dwarf angrily.

At that moment there was a loud growling and, lumbering across the meadow, with eyes glowering, came the great brown bear. The frightened dwarf jumped up, screaming, "Take these two wicked girls. They would be tastier than me."

But the huge bear swiped the cowardly dwarf with his paw. With one blow, the dwarf was motionless. The girls started to run but then they heard a familiar growl, "Snow-White, Rose-Red, it's me. Don't be afraid."

And as he spoke, the bearskin fell off, and there before the startled sisters stood a handsome prince in gold robes.

The happy prince returned to his castle and invited Snow-White and Rose-Red to visit him. The two sisters met the prince's younger brother, and all four soon became close friends.

Some time later, Snow-White married the prince and Rose-Red married his brother. The girls' mother came to live with them in the castle, where she had her own little garden. She planted two rose trees, and every year they produced beautiful roses, white and red.

The End

Thumbelina

There was once a poor woman who lived in a cottage. She had no husband, but she longed to have a child. One day, she visited a fairy to ask for her help.

"You are a good woman," said the fairy, "so I will give you this magic seed. Plant it and water it, and you will see what you will see."

The woman thanked the fairy and did as she was told. One day, then two days, then three days passed, and nothing happened. But on the fourth day, a tiny green shoot appeared. And on the fifth day, there was a flower bud, with glossy pink petals wrapped tightly around its center.

"What a beautiful flower you will be," smiled the woman, and she kissed it gently.

With that, the petals unfolded, and in the center of the flower was a beautiful girl, the size of a thumb. The woman clapped her hands with joy.

"I will call you Thumbelina," she cried, and she laid her new child in a walnut-shell bed with a rose-petal quilt.

Thumbelina was very happy with her mother.

Then one day, while her mother was away, an ugly, slimy toad crawled into the cottage. When she saw Thumbelina sleeping in the bed, she cried, "You'd be the perfect wife for my son!" She grabbed the girl and crept out of the cottage the same way she had come.

When Thumbelina woke up, she was sitting on a lily pad in the middle of a stream, with two warty toads staring at her.

"This is your new wife!" the mother said to her son. He opened his wide, toothless mouth in a grin, but all he could say was, **"Croak! Croak!"**

"I don't want to marry a toad," said Thumbelina, and she started to cry.

"You ungrateful girl!" the mother toad scolded her. "You'll stay here until you stop crying." The two toads jumped into the water and swam away. Thumbelina sobbed and sobbed.

Then, a fish took pity on her and nibbled through the lily pad's stem until it floated free. Thumbelina sailed gently downstream and escaped from the toads.

At last, she drifted to the riverbank and climbed onto dry land. Suddenly, a big brown beetle grabbed her with his claws.

"Put me down!" said Thumbelina.

"No," said the beetle. "You must stay with me and be my friend."

The beetle carried Thumbelina to a clearing. Another bigger, browner beetle was waiting for him there. He looked at Thumbelina and shook his head.

"Oh, Bertie, she's so ugly," said the bigger beetle. "She can't stay here!"

The two beetles argued and argued, waving their claws in the air, and pulling poor Thumbelina this way and that, until at last Bertie gave in and they let Thumbelina go. She ran off as fast as she could.

Thumbelina lived in the country all summer long. She missed her mother, but had no idea how to find her way home. So she busied herself collecting wild berries and making friends with the birds and small creatures she met.

Then winter came. Thumbelina was cold and hungry and all alone. Luckily, a kindly field mouse found her and invited her to stay with him in his burrow. She was so grateful that she said yes at once.

Life underground was warm and snug, but Thumbelina soon missed the sunshine. And then Mouse's friend Mole asked her to marry him.

"I don't want to marry a mole," cried Thumbelina. "And though I like living with you, Mouse, I miss the sunshine."

"You ungrateful girl!" said the mouse and the mole, together. So Thumbelina sadly agreed to marry the mole and a date was set for the following summer.

Thumbelina was miserable. Then one day, as she walked through the underground tunnels, she found a swallow, almost dead with the cold. She hugged the bird against herself to warm him. He slowly opened his eyes.

"You have saved my life," said the swallow. "Come with me to the South, to the land of sunshine and flowers."

"I cannot leave Mouse," sighed Thumbelina, "he has been so kind to me."

"Then I must go alone," said the swallow, stretching his wings, "but I will return next summer. Goodbye!" Then he flew away.

Months passed, and the day Thumbelina had been dreading arrived—the day she would marry the mole. As she waited for Mole to arrive, the swallow appeared again.

"Come with me now!" he cried.

"I will!" said Thumbelina.

So Thumbelina flew away to the South with the swallow. As she explored her new home, one especially beautiful flower opened in front of her. There, in the center, was a fairy prince, no bigger than a thumb, with butterfly wings.

"Will you be my wife?" he asked at once.

"I will!" cried Thumbelina.

So Thumbelina, wearing butterfly wings made especially for her, married the prince and became Queen of the flower fairies. She did not forget her mother, and that very day arranged for fairy messengers to deliver a letter to her and a bouquet of the most beautiful flowers. And kind Thumbelina and her handsome husband lived happily ever after.

The End

The Cat That Walked by Himself

At the very beginning of time, wild animals lived in the Wet Wild Woods and the wildest of all was the Cat. He walked by himself, waving his wild tail.

One night, Wild Dog asked Cat to go with him to the cave where Man and Woman lived. But the Cat replied, "I am the Cat who walks by himself, and all places are alike to me."

As Wild Dog set off, Wild Cat was curious, and so he followed him, taking care not to be seen.

When he reached the cave, Wild Dog said to the Woman, "What is this that smells so good?"

And the Woman threw him a lamb bone. It was so delicious he begged for another. So the Woman said, "Help my Man hunt through the day and guard this cave at night, and I will give you as many roast bones as you need."

Later, when the Man saw the Dog, the Woman said, "Take him with you when you go hunting as he is our friend."

Wild Cat was listening all the time and thought, "This is a very wise Woman, but she is not as wise as I am."

The next day the Wild Horse asked Wild Cat to help him search for Wild Dog. Now the Cat was eager to see what had happened to Wild Dog, but because he didn't want Wild Horse to know this, he replied, "I am the Cat who walks by himself."

So Wild Horse set off alone, not realizing that the Cat was following him.

When the Woman saw the Wild Horse, she laughed. "Wild Thing, you did not come here for Wild Dog, but for the sake of this dried grass." And then she promised him lots of wonderful grass if he wore a harness on his wild head.

And later she told the Man, "This Servant will carry us from place to place. Ride on his back when you go hunting."

Hearing this, the Wild Cat was even more impressed with how clever the Woman was.

It was Wild Cow's turn to visit the cave next. Wild Cow promised milk every day in return for the lush green grass. So the Woman agreed and later explained to the Man that the cow would provide food for them.

Listening once again, the Cat decided he should talk to the Woman himself.

So the next day, Cat visited the Woman and told her, "I am not a friend, and I am not a servant. I am the Cat who walks by himself, and I wish to come into your cave."

The clever Woman bargained with him, "I will give you warm milk three times a day for always but only if you do three things to earn my praise."

And the Cat replied, "The Curtain, the Fire, and the Milk-pots will see that you keep your promise." Then the Cat returned alone to the Wild Woods.

Some time later, the Cat heard there was a baby in the cave. "Ah," he said, "my time has come."

When he reached the cave, the Woman was busy spinning and the Baby was crying. The Cat patted the Baby with his paw, and he cooed; then he tickled him under his fat chin with his tail. And the Baby laughed.

Not seeing the Cat, the Woman was relieved that some creature had stopped her Baby from crying. "What a gentle Thing!" she said.

Now the Curtain heard the Woman's praise and immediately fell down. When she found the Wild Cat underneath the Curtain, the Woman was very angry and sent the Cat away.

Later as the Baby started to cry again, the Cat crept back in and whispered, "I will show you a magic trick." Then he tied some thread to a piece of wood and chased it across the floor. The Baby laughed as much as he had been crying.

"Clever Cat," said the woman gratefully.

The fire heard the Woman praise the Cat and gave a great puff! The Woman was not pleased to see the Cat now sitting comfortably by her fireside. But when a little mouse ran across the floor, she jumped up on the footstool, quivering, until the Cat chased the mouse away.

"Thank you," she said. "You were very quick."

Now this was the third time the Woman had praised the Cat, and the Milk-pot remembered her promise to provide the cat with milk. So the Milk-pot cracked in two, and soon the Cat was lapping up the warm milk.

That evening, the Man also made
a bargain with the Cat.
    "You can stay only if you catch mice
in the cave. If you fail, I will throw you
out of the cave, and so shall all Men."
    Then the Dog bargained with the cat, too.
"If you are not kind to the Baby I will chase
you up a tree. And so shall all dogs after me."
    And so the Cat keeps his side of the
bargain, for as long as the Baby doesn't pull
his tail too hard. He will kill mice and be
kind to the Baby when he is in the house.
But between times, and when night comes,
        he is the Cat that walks by himself,
        and all places are alike to him.

The End

The Boy Who Cried Wolf

Once upon a time, there was a boy named Peter who lived in a little village in the mountains with his parents, who were sheep farmers. It was Peter's job to watch over the flock and protect the sheep from wolves.

Day after day, Peter sat on the mountainside watching the flock. It was very quiet with no one but sheep for company. No wolves ever came to eat the sheep.

Peter got very bored. He tried to amuse himself by climbing rocks and trees or by crawling through the grass and counting the sheep, one by one.

"One, two, three ... sixty-four, sixty-five ..." counted Peter, "Oh, I wish something exciting would happen. I'm so bored! Same old mountain, same old sheep ..."

Finally, one day, Peter couldn't stand being bored any more. "I know what to do!" he grinned to himself.

He started shouting at the top of his voice, "Wolf! Help! Wolf!"

Down in the village, a man heard Peter's cries.

"Quick!" he shouted to some other men. "We need to help Peter. There's a big wolf attacking the sheep."

The villagers grabbed their axes, forks, shovels, and brooms and ran up the mountain to where Peter was shepherding his flock.

When they got there, puffing and panting, all was quiet and the sheep were grazing peacefully.

"Where's the wolf?" one of the villagers cried.

Peter roared with laughter. "There's no wolf. I was just playing!"

The men were very angry with Peter. "You mustn't cry wolf when there isn't one," they said.

That night Peter got a telling-off from his mother and was sent to bed without any supper.

For a while after this, Peter managed to behave himself. He climbed the mountainside with the sheep every day and watched over them quietly. The villagers soon forgot about his trick.

Then one day, Peter got really bored again. He had already run up and down the rocks, climbed three trees, and counted the sheep ten times.

"What can I do now? Same old mountain, same old sheep ..." he groaned to himself.

With a sigh, he slumped to the ground. As he was sitting there, an idea popped into his head. He picked up some sticks lying nearby and started banging them hard together. Then at the top of his voice, he shouted, "Wolf! Help! Wolf! Please hurry, there's a big wolf eating the sheep!"

Down in the village, a crowd of people started gathering when they heard the loud banging and shouting coming from the mountainside.

"What's all that noise?" someone cried.

"It's Peter. He's in trouble!" shouted someone else. "Quick, there must be a wolf on the prowl."

Once again, the villagers grabbed their forks, shovels, and brooms. They ran up the mountain to chase away the wolf and save poor Peter and his sheep.

And once again, when they got there, puffing and out of breath, all was quiet and the sheep were grazing peacefully.

"Peter, what's happened?" shouted one man angrily.

"There's no wolf," laughed Peter. "I was only playing."

"You shouldn't make jokes like that," said another man. "It's not good to lie." The villagers marched back down the mountain toward the village.

That night, Peter got an even bigger telling-off from his mother and once again had to go to bed without any supper.

For a few days, the villagers
went around moaning about
Peter and his tricks. But after a
while the incident was forgotten, and Peter
continued to climb the mountainside every day
with the sheep.

He had decided that he would try and behave
himself, especially as he didn't want another scolding
from his mother.

A few weeks later, while Peter stood counting the sheep as
usual to pass the time, he noticed that some of them were bleating
nervously. He climbed up a tree to take a look around and see
what was upsetting them.

To his horror, he saw a big hairy wolf. The terrifying
creature was creeping through the grass toward the
flock with its jaws open and its long
tongue hanging out. Peter could
see the wolf's sharp,
pointed teeth.

Shaking with fear, he started screaming, "Wolf! Help! Wolf! Please hurry, there's a big wolf about to eat the sheep!"

A few people down in the village heard his cries for help, but they kept on with their business as usual. "It's only Peter playing another trick," they said to each other. "Does he think he can fool us again?"

And so nobody went to Peter's rescue.

By nightfall, when Peter hadn't returned, his parents became concerned. Peter never missed his supper—something bad must have happened.

Peter's father gathered the people of the village, and together they hurried up the mountain, carrying flaming torches.

A terrible sight met their eyes. All the sheep were gone! There really had been a wolf this time.

Peter was still in the tree, shaking and crying.

"I cried out wolf! Why didn't you come?" he wept.

"Nobody believes a liar, even when he's speaking the truth," said Peter's father, helping him climb out of the tree. Peter hung on to his father all the way home. He never wanted to see another wolf ever again.

And Peter finally really learnt his lesson. He never told a lie again, and he always got to eat his supper.

The End

The Twelve Dancing Princesses

There was once a king who had twelve beautiful daughters. They slept in one room, and every night their father would lock their door. But every morning there were twelve pairs of worn-out dancing shoes under their beds. It was as if the princesses had been out all night dancing. But how could that be? It was a mystery no one could solve except the princesses, and they simply smiled whenever they were asked.

"Any man who discovers the secret of where the princesses go at night," proclaimed the king, "shall have one of my daughters in marriage. But," he warned, "anyone who fails after three nights will be punished by death."

Many suitors tried, but all failed to uncover the secret of the twelve princesses.

Now it happened that a soldier was passing through the kingdom when he met an old woman. Hearing that he would like to be the one to solve the mystery, the woman gave him some advice.

"When one of the princesses offers you some wine," she said, "pretend to drink it and then act as if you are sleeping deeply." And handing him a special cloak, she explained, "Wear this and you will become invisible so you can follow the princesses."

Later that night when the king had locked the door of the princesses' bedroom, the eldest princess gave the soldier a goblet of wine. Carefully pouring it away, he soon pretended to snore loudly.

"We have tricked another one!" laughed the princess as they all changed into their ballgowns and tied their new dancing shoes.

Then as the eldest princess clapped her hands, a trap door magically opened up beneath her feet. One by one the twelve princesses disappeared down the steps. The soldier immediately sprang up and grabbed the cloak. Just as the old woman had predicted, he now became invisible. But in his haste, he stepped on the hem of the dress of the youngest princess.

"Someone has pulled my dress," she cried.

"Don't be silly," replied one of her sisters, "it's just a nail."

At the bottom of the stairs, a door opened out to a spectacular avenue of trees, each one bearing silver leaves that shimmered under the starlit sky.

Following closely behind the laughing princesses, the invisible soldier broke off a silver branch, which snapped loudly.

"See, we are being followed," cried the youngest princess. But her sisters were too excited to worry.

Leaving the silver trees behind, the happy princesses now ran daintily through an avenue of pure gold trees. It was a magnificent sight in the moonlight.

The soldier followed, snapping off a golden branch. Finally they reached the glittering diamond trees, and to the invisible soldier, this was the most breathtaking sight of all. As the soldier snapped off a branch from a diamond tree, the youngest princess screamed, but her sisters only laughed more loudly as they ran toward the lake. Lined up on the water were twelve little boats, and in each was a prince ready to row the princesses across to the castle. The soldier jumped into the boat with the youngest princess as the sound of trumpets filled the air.

Inside the castle, music and laughter rang out as the princesses danced with their handsome princes in the ballroom. The youngest princess was the only one feeling uneasy all evening. Every time she lifted a goblet of wine, it was snatched out of her hand by the mischievous soldier. She tried in vain to warn her sisters, but they were only interested in having fun. They danced and danced until finally the cock crowed. Then the twelve princes rowed them back across the lake.

The soldier managed to run ahead and was back in bed snoring when the princesses returned to their room.

"We're safe!" whispered the eldest sister checking up on the sleeping soldier. Happy but tired, the twelve princesses took off their tattered dancing shoes and were soon fast asleep.

The soldier followed the princesses again the next night, and on the third night he took a golden goblet from the castle as proof of where the sisters had been. So when he was summoned to the king after the final night, he was able to show him a silver branch, a gold branch, and a diamond branch, as well as the castle goblet. The princesses' secret had finally been discovered. The grateful king kept his promise.

"Which of the princesses will you choose for your wife?" he asked the soldier.

"I am not a young man, Sir," replied the soldier, "so I think I will choose the eldest."

Soon they were married, and in time the soldier became king of the whole country. He ruled wisely and never forgot the old woman in the woods and her words of advice.

The End

The Town Mouse
and the Country Mouse

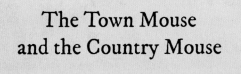

Once upon a time, there were two little mice. One of them lived in the town, and the other one lived in the country.

One day, the Town Mouse went to visit the Country Mouse. He had never been to the country before, so he was very excited. He packed a small suitcase and went on his way.

Country Mouse's home was small and dark—not at all like Town Mouse's home. Lunch was very different, too. There was creamy cheese, juicy apples, and crispy, crunchy hazelnuts. It was all very tasty, but when Town Mouse had finished, he was still hungry.

After lunch, Country Mouse took Town Mouse for a walk. They went down a sunny path, through a creaky gate and into a large field. Town Mouse was just starting to enjoy himself when ...

"Moo!"

"What was that?" he asked nervously,
scurrying closer to Country Mouse.

"Ha! That's just a cow," said his friend. "There are lots of them in
the country. It's nothing to be scared of."

Town Mouse and Country Mouse strolled on, through a flowery
meadow and over a grassy hill. Soon, they came to a peaceful pond.
Town Mouse was just starting to enjoy himself when ...

"Hiss!"

"What was that?" he asked again, quivering from nose to tail.

"Ha! That's just a goose," said his friend. "There are lots of
them in the country. It's nothing to be scared of."

Town Mouse and Country Mouse kept on walking, across a rickety bridge, down a sandy track, and into a shady forest. Town Mouse was just starting to enjoy himself when ...

"Twit-twoo!"

"What was that?" he yelped, and he jumped off the ground in terror.

"It's an owl!" cried Country Mouse. "Run for your life! If it catches you, it will eat you up!"

So the two mice ran and ran until they found a leafy hedge to hide in.

Town Mouse was terrified. "I don't like the country at all!" he said. "Come to stay with me in the town. You'll see how much better it is!"

Country Mouse had never been to the town before, so he packed a small rucksack and went to stay with his friend.

Town Mouse's home was huge and grand, not at all like Country Mouse's home.

Lunch was very different, too! Instead of apples and nuts, there were sandwiches and cupcakes and chocolates. Lots and lots of them. It was tasty, but soon Country Mouse began to feel a bit ill.

After dinner, the friends went out for a walk. They walked past shops and offices and houses. Country Mouse was just starting to enjoy himself when ...

"Beep-beep!"

"What's that?" he asked fearfully, looking about him.

"That? It's just a car," said his friend. "There are lots of them in the town. It's nothing to be afraid of."

Then the mice walked through a park, past a church, and down a wide road. Country Mouse was just starting to enjoy himself when ...

"Nee-nah! Nee-nah!"

"What's that?" he asked again, his whiskers twitching.

"That? It's just a fire engine. There are lots of them in the town. It's nothing to be afraid of."

As the mice pitter-pattered home they passed a playground, a school, and a pretty garden. Country Mouse was just starting to enjoy himself when ...

"Meow!"

"What's that?" he squeaked, his eyes as wide as saucers.

"It's a cat!" cried Town Mouse. "Run for your life! If it catches you, it will eat you up!"

So the two mice ran and ran, all the way back to Town Mouse's home.

Country Mouse was terrified! "I don't like the town at all! I'm going home," he said.

"But how can you be happy living near the cow and the goose and that horrible owl?" said Town Mouse.

"They don't scare me!" cried Country Mouse. "How can you be happy living near the cars and the fire engines and that terrible cat?"

"They don't scare me!" cried Town Mouse.

The two mice looked at each other. Who was right and who was wrong? They would simply never agree. So they shook hands and went their separate ways: Town Mouse to his grand home and Country Mouse to his cozy one.

"Home, sweet home!" said the Town Mouse, sighing a deep, happy sigh.

"Home, sweet home!" said the Country Mouse, smiling a big, happy smile.

And the two of them lived happily ever after, each in his own way.

The End

The Goose That Laid the Golden Egg

There was a farmer and his wife who worked very hard but never had much to eat. The crops did not grow as well as on other farms, and their animals never seemed to fatten up. You could see the bones on the cows, and even the pigs were scrawny.

So, every day in the morning, the poor couple had just a little bit
of bread and a couple of glasses of thin milk. For dinner they had just
the one goose egg between them. Indeed, their goose egg dinner was
their only treat of the day. If there was a morning when the goose
failed to lay an egg, they had to go without dinner that evening. But,
fortunately, this rarely happened.

"She's a good goose," the farmer told his wife as he cut his half of
egg into thin slices. That way it went farther. The goose eggs were
always delicious, firm, and white on the outside and rich and yellow
on the inside.

"Yes," the wife agreed. "She's a very good goose, even though we
can't afford to feed her much."

There were times when the farmer and his wife envied the other farmers, who had all sorts of fine foods for their dinner.

"If I were rich," said the farmer, "I would have roast beef every day."

"And if I were rich," said the wife, "I would throw away my old clothes and buy myself a beautiful new dress."

Of course, they both knew this was never likely to happen, and they expected to be poor until the end of their days.

Yet one morning, as the wife put her hand in the hay to collect the goose egg, her heart nearly stopped. The egg felt particularly hard and shiny. She immediately thought something was wrong with the goose.

A few moments later, she was excitedly running across the fields in search of her husband.

"Come quickly!" she cried. "The goose has laid a golden egg!"

"That can't be true," the farmer said when she had at last found him. Then she showed him the golden egg. The delighted farmer lifted his wife into the air, and they danced around the kitchen.

The couple wasted no time in making the long walk into town to check that the egg really was made of gold. An old jeweler paid them a very handsome price for it, and so the wife was able to buy the beautiful dress she had always dreamed of. They returned home in a fine horse and carriage!

The next morning, they were delighted to see that the goose had laid another golden egg. And it laid another the day after that. In fact, it seemed that the goose could only lay golden eggs now.

"We must do everything we can to take care of the goose," the wife said. "We need to make its cage much stronger so foxes or thieves don't take it. When word gets round about our goose that lays golden eggs, lots of people will try to steal it!"

They had the money now to take care of the goose properly, and they built the strongest, grandest cage imaginable. They also fed it the very best corn and bought it the finest hay to lay its special eggs on. All this attention worked, because the goose continued to lay golden eggs day after day. And the farmer and his wife became richer and richer.

In spite of this, they started to wonder how to make even more money.

"Maybe if we fed the goose twice as much corn," the farmer suggested, "then it would lay two eggs a day instead of just one."

Sure enough, after giving the goose the extra corn, the next morning there were two shiny golden eggs lying in the cage. So they fed the goose three times as much corn a day, then four times. The more it was fed, the more golden eggs it laid.

But one morning they woke to find the goose writhing in pain, lying in the corner of the cage.

"We've overfed it!" the wife wailed. "Oh, why were we so greedy! Why couldn't we be content with just one golden egg a day?"

They did everything they could to revive the goose, nursing it day and night.

Finally, one morning the goose rose shakily to its feet. It was well again. It even laid an egg. But it was just an ordinary egg, not a golden one. In fact, the goose never laid another golden egg. And the farmer and his wife were never greedy again. They were just happy with what they had.

The End

The Emperor's New Clothes

Once upon a time, there lived an emperor who really loved clothes. He would strut around his palace in different outfits, day and night. There were mirrors in every room so he could admire his reflection as he passed by.

The emperor had outfits for the morning ...

... and different outfits for the afternoon ...

... and extra special outfits for the evening made from the most expensive cloth and sewn with pure gold thread.

In fact, the emperor had so many clothes that he often didn't know what to wear!

One day, two wicked men called at the palace. They knew all about the emperor's love of clothes.

"Your Highness, we are weavers," they said. "But we can do something that no other weavers can do. We can make a magic cloth. This cloth is very special because only very clever people can see it."

The emperor was impressed. "I would like you to make me a suit from this magic cloth," he said.

"Of course, Your Highness, it would be an honor," said the first weaver.

"Sire, we will need lots of gold thread," said the second weaver.

"You shall have all the gold thread you need," replied the emperor. He turned to one of his servants. "Please show these fine gentlemen to the royal storeroom."

The two men had never seen so much gold thread. Laughing and clapping their hands with glee, they filled their bags, and left the palace.

A few days later the emperor called for one of his ministers.

"Go and find out how the weavers are getting on," he ordered impatiently. "I need something new to wear."

The minister went off to the weavers' workshop. There he found the two weavers sitting in front of a loom, busy at work.

The minister rubbed his eyes. He couldn't see any cloth on the loom.

"That's strange," he thought. Not wanting to appear foolish, he smiled at the weavers.

"The cloth is looking wonderful. When will the emperor's suit be ready?" he asked.

"Soon, soon," replied the first weaver.

"But we will need more gold thread to complete the suit," said the second weaver.

The minister hurried back to the emperor. As soon as he had gone, the weavers roared with laughter.

"Oh, this is priceless! What a foolish man!"

Back at the palace, the minister bowed before the emperor. Not wishing to be called a fool he said, "Sire, I have never seen a cloth more beautiful. The weavers need more gold thread to finish your suit."

"Well, send more over then," replied the emperor.

For a whole week the weavers pretended to cut and sew the magic cloth to make the new suit. At last they returned to the palace, proudly pretending to carry the cloth.

The emperor was very excited and handed the weavers a bag of gold coins to pay for the outfit. He took off his clothes and the weavers fussed around him, pretending to smooth and adjust the suit.

"It fits you perfectly!" they cried.

The emperor looked in the mirror. He couldn't see any clothes, but not wanting to appear foolish, he said, "It's wonderful!"

As soon as the two men had left the palace, they doubled over with laughter. Their cunning plan had worked.

News of the emperor's suit quickly spread throughout the kingdom. Everyone was sure they would be able to see the magic cloth.

"Yes, Sire, truly splendid!" agreed the emperor's ministers.

No matter how hard he looked, the emperor still could not see any clothes.

"I can't be more of a fool than my ministers," he thought, "and they can all see the suit." So he smiled at the weavers and thanked them once again.

The vain emperor sent out a royal announcement. He would lead a grand procession through the city wearing his new suit.

When the great day arrived, the emperor sent for the two weavers to help him get dressed.

"Ah, Your Highness, you do look wonderful," they cried.

People had gathered in the streets to catch a glimpse of the emperor as the procession passed by. Finally the emperor appeared riding on a fine white horse. Nervous whispers rippled through the crowd. No one wanted to appear foolish, so at last a timid voice called out, "The emperor's new clothes are magnificent!"

Suddenly everyone started talking and shouting at once.

"How stylish!"

"Smart and fashionable!"

The emperor smiled as he trotted along, feeling very pleased with himself. Then a small boy and his sister pushed to the front of the crowd. They started to point and giggle.

"Look!" they cried. "The emperor has no clothes on!"

Suddenly, everyone knew that it was true. Before long the laughter had spread through the crowd.

The emperor turned bright red.

"What a fool I am!" he gasped. "How could I have been so silly and vain?" He looked around for the two weavers, but of course they were nowhere to be seen.

Filled with shame, the emperor made his way back to the palace to get dressed.

"I will never be so vain about my clothes again," said the emperor to his minister.

He was true to his word—and he was a much happier emperor from that day on.

The End

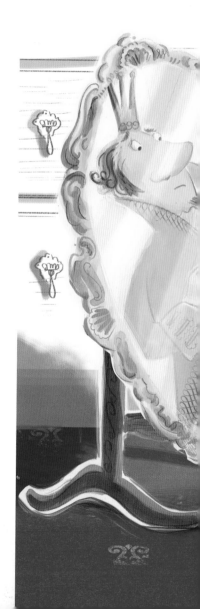

The Fox and the Crow

Most crows would accept that they are not the most striking birds. However, there was one crow who always sulked when the other woodland birds chatted about who was the most colorful or who had the finest voice. So she was not happy when a baby bird suddenly chirped, "Who has the most beautiful feathers?"

Before anyone could say a word, the crow answered, "The crow, of course."

Now the other birds laughed so much, the branches all swayed.

"Nonsense, everyone knows the kingfisher has the most beautiful orange and blue feathers," said the sparrow. "A crow is just the same dull color from head to toe. Even the blackbird has orange feet."

"Well, who can sing the best then?" asked the baby bird.

And without hesitation the crow replied confidently, "The crow, of course."

This time some of the birds were knocked out of the tree, which shook from the laughter of all the birds.

"No, no!" chuckled the woodpecker. "It's the nightingale who has the sweetest song. A crow's voice is too croaky and makes me think of winter."

The crow was so upset, she wanted to fly off to be on her own. She hung her head in shame, but then suddenly spied a large piece of cheese lying in the grass below.

"I do have a good voice," she told herself, "and I'm clever. None of the others have spotted that cheese." And she swooped down, grabbing the cheese with her sharp beak.

Then she flew back to the tree, flapping her wings proudly, showing off her prize to the envy of all the other birds.

"What a lovely piece of cheese," cried the sparrow. "Can we share it?"

But the crow shook her head. After all, why should she share when everyone had been so mean to her? So the other birds all flew away in disgust.

"Good," thought the crow, "now I can enjoy my cheese in peace." She flew up to a higher branch and settled herself.

But just at that moment, a beautiful red fox sauntered by. Spotting the crow, his eyes narrowed as he saw the cheese wedged in her beak.

"Mm, mm," thought the fox, "that looks a tasty piece of cheese, indeed. I must have it." Now the fox knew he needed a clever plan. So he slowly circled the tree twice before deciding what to do.

Seeing the fox, a family of rabbits quickly ran from the woods and into the meadow to hide. They knew exactly how dangerous he could be.

"Good morning," said the fox in his friendliest voice, calling up to the crow. "What a very fine bird you are! Look at your glossy feathers, how they shine. You must be the finest bird I have ever seen." And noticing the crow raising her head up high, he added, "None of the other birds in the woods is a match for you."

This is just what the crow needed to hear. No one had ever told her she had beautiful feathers. In fact no one had ever admired anything about her before.

"I am beautiful, too," she said to herself as she brimmed with pride.

The fox had hoped the crow would open her mouth to say thank you. So far, his plan was not working. He needed to think quickly.

"I imagine a bird with fine sleek feathers like you would also have a beautiful voice," he continued, using all his cunning.

The delighted crow nodded. "At last," she thought, "here is someone who appreciates me. All those other birds who think I have a croaky voice are plain wrong! I wish they could hear what this fox is telling me."

The fox was losing patience but tried once more.

"Would you be so kind as to share your beautiful voice with me?" he asked meekly. "I'm sure it's even sweeter than the song of the nightingale."

And this time the crow couldn't resist the fox's flattery.

"I do have a beautiful voice," she told herself. "And I'm going to prove it," she added defiantly. She puffed up her chest and opened her sharp beak.

"Caw! Caw! C–!" she croaked.

Down! Down! Down fell the cheese. Right into the fox's wide-open mouth. **SNAP!** went his jaws. The fox chewed the cheese very slowly, determined to enjoy every little bite. This was surely the best cheese he had ever tasted.

"So good!" he called up to the stunned crow. And as he slinked away he added, "You really are a very vain bird. A very vain bird who can't sing either."

As the crow sat on the branch all alone, she realized she had learned a very important lesson today. And she knew she would never be fooled by flattery ever again.

The End

The Sorcerer's Apprentice

Once upon a time, a young boy named Franz went to work as an apprentice for a sorcerer. The sorcerer lived in a huge castle overlooking the little village where Franz lived with his family. It was considered a great honor to help and learn from such a clever and powerful man.

Franz was very excited about learning how to do magic. But when he arrived on his first day, he was just given a long list of chores to do around the castle—cleaning, tidying up, and fetching water from the well.

Franz was not happy. "It's not fair!" he muttered to himself. "I didn't come here to be his servant. When will I get to do some magic?"

The sorcerer was a busy man. Each morning he would tell his apprentice what chores needed doing that day. He would then disappear into his workshop in the castle or journey out to one of the surrounding villages in the area, leaving Franz alone.

Occasionally, as Franz went about the castle doing his chores, he would catch a glimpse of the great sorcerer looking through the pages of a large leather-bound book, which he kept locked in a wooden cabinet in his workshop. The pages of this book were filled with beautiful illustrations and the words of the sorcerer's magic spells. Franz longed to have a look in the book himself.

Several months later,
fed up with just doing chores
all day, Franz decided he would
sneak a look in the sorcerer's
special spell book when the old
man was gone.

As the sorcerer got ready to
leave the castle that day, he
called out to Franz.

"Boy, I need you to scrub the
floor of the Great Hall for me,"
he said. "You will need to fetch
water from the well with this
bucket, and carry it to the big
stone container in the hall."

Franz rolled his eyes behind
the sorcerer's back. "Of course,
sir," he mumbled.

"When the container is full of
water," continued the sorcerer,
"take the broom and give the
floor a good scrub. I want to see
it shining when I get back
this afternoon."

As soon as the sorcerer left, Franz climbed the small staircase to the workshop. He knew where the sorcerer kept the key to the wooden cabinet, so he grabbed it and hurriedly opened the old, creaking doors. Inside, on a shelf, sat the magic spell book.

Franz carried the heavy book to the Great Hall and sat down to look through its magical pages. There were spells for all sorts of weird and wonderful things.

As he turned the pages, Franz saw a spell that could bring any object to life. This gave him a brilliant idea.

"What harm can one little spell do?" he thought to himself.

Grinning, Franz rushed to fetch the broom and bucket. He placed the broom on the floor, sat back down at the desk and slowly chanted the words of the magic spell. He couldn't wait to see the broom clean the Great Hall by itself!

At first nothing happened. Franz was just about to try the spell again, when suddenly the broom sprouted little arms and leapt up from the floor. Franz was so surprised he nearly fell off his chair!

This was amazing. He was doing magic!

"Broom!" he commanded. "Take the bucket to the well and fetch water to fill that container."

The broom marched off to the well and started carrying the bucket backward and forward between the well and the container in the Great Hall.

Franz couldn't believe his eyes. Laughing as the little broom kept bringing the water, he cried, "I am the master! And you must obey me!"

After a while, Franz noticed that the container was overflowing and that the water was running all over the floor.

"Stop, little broom!" he shouted. The broom, however, kept on fetching water.

"What am I to do now?" thought Franz. Flipping through the pages of the magic book, he tried to find a spell to make the broom stop.

But the broom kept on going. By now the water was all over the floor. Franz grabbed an ax and chopped the broom into small pieces.

"That should do it," he said with a sigh of relief.

To his dismay, the little pieces of broom started to move and grow, and they too sprouted arms and legs. Soon there was an army of new brooms. They all began to march to the well to fetch more water.

Franz didn't know what to do! The brooms continued splashing the water into the Great Hall, and soon it was swirling around Franz's knees. He was powerless to stop the brooms.

Just then, the sorcerer returned. He raised his arms, and in a booming voice, chanted a magic spell. In an instant the brooms all vanished and the water disappeared. Everything returned to normal.

Shaking with fear, Franz fell to his knees. "Please forgive me, master," he begged. "I just wanted to try some magic."

The sorcerer was very angry. "Never play with things you don't understand!" he shouted. "Magic is very powerful and should only be used by a sorcerer."

Franz hung his head in shame. He would never get the chance to learn magic now.

"I should send you away, boy," continued the sorcerer, but he could see that Franz was very sorry. He decided to give him another chance.

"You can stay," he said. "You still have much training to complete."

Franz was so relieved. "Thank you, sir!" he said. "I promise I will work very hard."

"Well," said the sorcerer, "you can start by cleaning this floor—the old-fashioned way!"

The End

The Ugly Duckling

Once upon a time, there was a proud and happy duck. "I have seven beautiful eggs, and soon I will have seven beautiful ducklings," she told the other creatures of the riverbank.

It wasn't long before she heard a **CRACK!** And one beautiful duckling popped her little head out of the shell.

"Isn't she a beauty!" she exclaimed. Soon there was another ... and then another ... until she had six beautiful little ducklings, drying their fluffy yellow wings in the spring air.

"Just one egg left,"
quacked Mother Duck,
"and it's a big one!" For quite
a while, nothing happened.
Mother Duck was starting to
worry when, at last, the big egg
began to hatch.

Tap, tap, tap! Out came a beak.

Crack, crack, crack! Out popped a head.

Crunch, crunch, crunch! Out came the last duckling.

"Oh, my!" said Mother Duck. "Isn't he ... different!"

The last duckling did look strange. He was bigger than the
other ducklings and didn't have such lovely yellow feathers.

"That's all right," said Mother Duck. "You're my special little
duckling. Now come on into the water," she told her little ones.
"You must learn to swim right away." One by one, the ducklings
hopped into the water, landing with a little plop. But the ugly
duckling fell over his big feet and landed in the water with a
great big **SPLASH!** The other ducklings laughed at their clumsy
brother.

"Now, my little chicks," said Mother Duck, "stick together and
stay behind me!"

Back at the nest, the ducklings practiced their quacking.

"Repeat after me," said their mother. "Quack, quack, quackety-quack!"

"Quack, quack, quackety-quack!" repeated the ducklings, all except for the ugly one.

"Honk! Honk!" he called. However much he tried, he couldn't quack like his brothers and sisters.

"What a racket!" said Mother Duck. "I'm sure you'll get the hang of it soon enough."

The other ducklings all quacked with laughter.

The ugly duckling hung his head in shame.

"Nobody likes me," he thought. "I'll never fit in."

The next day, the mother duck took her little ones out for another swim. Once again, the little ducklings stayed close to her while the ugly duckling wandered alone. Some wild geese came swooping down and landed on the river nearby.

"What kind of a bird are you?" asked one goose, rather rudely.

"I'm a duckling, of course," he replied. "My family have left me all alone."

The rest of the geese felt sorry for the ugly duckling.

"Come away with us," they said. "It's a big wide world, and there's so much to see!" But the ugly duckling was afraid to leave his river, so he stayed where he was.

When their mother wasn't looking, the other ducklings teased their ugly brother.

"Just look at his dull, gray feathers," said his sister unkindly, as she admired her own reflection in the water. "Mine are so much prettier!"

The ugly duckling swam away and looked at his reflection.

"I don't look the same as them," he thought.

Feeling sad and lonely, he swam down the river and didn't stop until he'd reached a place he had never seen before. "I may as well stay here by myself," he decided.

Summer turned to autumn. The sky became cloudy and the river murky. But still the ugly duckling swam alone in his quiet part of the river.

Snow fell heavily that winter, and the ugly duckling was cold and lonely. The river was frozen solid.

"At least, I can't see my ugly reflection any more," he thought to himself.

Spring arrived at last and the ice thawed. New visitors arrived on the river. The ugly duckling watched nervously as some magnificent white ducks swam toward him.

"You're very big ducks," he told them, when they swam close.

"We're not ducks," laughed the elegant creatures. "We're swans—just like you!"

The ugly duckling didn't know what they meant. He looked at his reflection in the river and was surprised to see beautiful white feathers and an elegant long neck.

"Is that really me?" he asked, surprised.

"Of course it is," they told him. "You are a truly handsome swan!"

The handsome young swan joined his new friends and glided gracefully back up the river with them.

When he swam past a family of ducks, Mother Duck recognized her ugly duckling right away.

"I always knew he was special," she said.

And the beautiful young swan swam down the river proudly, ruffling his magnificent white feathers and holding his elegant head high.

The End

Index